Spring's Gentle Promise

SEASONS OF THE HEART #4

JANETTE OKE

Spring's Gentle Promise

BETHANY HOUSE
MINNEAPOLIS, MINNESOTA

Spring's Gentle Promise
Copyright © 1989
Janette Oke

Cover design by Dan Pitts
Cover photography by Aimee Christenson

Scripture quotations are taken from the King James Version of the Bible.

All rights reserved. No part of this publication may be reproduced, stored in a retrieval system, or transmitted in any form or by any means—electronic, mechanical, photocopying, recording, or otherwise—without the prior written permission of the publisher. The only exception is brief quotations in printed reviews.

Published by Bethany House Publishers
11400 Hampshire Avenue South
Bloomington, Minnesota 55438

Bethany House Publishers is a division of
Baker Publishing Group, Grand Rapids, Michigan.

Printed in the United States of America

Library of Congress Cataloging-in-Publication Data

Oke, Janette, 1935–
Spring's gentle promise / Janette Oke.
p. cm. — (Seasons of the heart ; 4)
Sequel to: Winter is not forever.
ISBN 978-0-7642-0803-4 (pbk.)
1. Orphans—Fiction. 2. Farm life—Fiction. 3. Depressions—1929—Fiction. 4. Domestic fiction. I. Title.
PR9199.3.O38S67 2010
813'.54—dc22

2010004160

To all the men and women
of the soil,
past and present,
who have fought against the elements
and the changing times
to maintain their roots
and to pass on a heritage.
We need you.
We cheer you on.
God bless you.

JANETTE OKE was born in Champion, Alberta, to a Canadian prairie farmer and his wife, and she grew up in a large family full of laughter and love. She is a graduate of Mountain View Bible College in Alberta, where she met her husband, Edward, and they were married in May of 1957. After pastoring churches in Indiana and Canada, the Okes spent some years in Calgary, where Edward served in several positions on college faculties while Janette continued her writing. She has written forty-eight novels for adults and another sixteen for children, and her book sales total nearly thirty million copies.

The Okes have three sons and one daughter, all married, and are enjoying their fifteen grandchildren. Edward and Janette are active in their local church and make their home near Didsbury, Alberta.

Contents

Characters

Joshua Chadwick Jones—The boy raised by his aunt Lou, grandfather, and great-uncle Charlie. Josh is now an adult, farming the family farm.

Grandpa and Uncle Charlie—The menfolk who share Josh's home and life.

Matilda—The neighborhood schoolteacher who boards with the Joneses.

Mary Turley—Housekeeper and neighbor girl who helps the men with the kitchen duties. In Grandpa's thinking, two girls in the house make the arrangement more "respectable."

Willie—Josh's boyhood friend who went to Africa as a missionary and died of a native disease.

Camellia—Josh's first love, but she loved Willie instead.

Chapter 1

A Beautiful Morning

I WAS WHISTLING AS I left the house. It was early. The sky had brightened, but the sun had not as yet lifted its head above the tree line that marked the border of the Sanders' place—new neighbors in our community.

Even in the dimness of early morning I could see field after neighborhood field as I let my gaze wander around me. First there was ours—I supposed I would always think of the farm as *ours*—Grandpa's, Uncle Charlie's and mine—though in truth it really was just mine now. Guess that was one of the reasons I was whistling. Just yesterday Grandpa and Uncle Charlie had signed all the official papers to make the farm mine—really and legally mine. *Joshua Chadwick Jones* the papers read, clear as could be. The full impact had yet to hit me. But I was excited. Really excited. I mean, what other fella my age had a farm of his own, title clear and paid for?

I sobered down a bit. It was a big responsibility 'cause I was the one who had to make the farm "bring forth" now. Had to support Grandpa and Uncle Charlie and myself and Mary, our housekeeper, and even Matilda, our boarder, though she did pay us some board and room.

I was the one who had to make the right decisions about which crops to plant and which field to plant them in, which livestock to sell and which ones to keep, and where to find the particular animal that would help build up the herd. I would need to keep up the fences, repaint the buildings, work the garden, keep the machinery in working order, watch out for weeds, put up the hay for winter feeding. . . . The list went on and on—but that didn't dim my spirits. It was a beautiful morning. I was a full-grown man with a place of my own.

I lengthened my stride. I'd been dawdling somewhat while I looked all around. The fields, the tree line, the wooded area where the crick passed through, the pastureland, and then the fields of the Turleys, Smiths, Sanders, the faraway hill that marked another Smith, the road to town—I knew it all. And I loved it more than I would ever have been able to say.

My roots were buried deep in this countryside I had known since a child. This was my life. My whole sense of being and knowing and living and growing were somehow wrapped up in the soil that stretched away before me.

I opened the gate at the end of the lane and took a break in my whistling to speak to the milk cows. The little jersey, one of my most recent purchases, rubbed her head against me gently as she moved to pass by. I reached out and ran my hand over her neck. She seemed satisfied then, and I smiled. *She's a great little cow,* I gloated. *Can fill the milk pail with the richest milk I've ever seen.* She was a mite spoiled though. Her former owners had treated her as the family pet.

I hurried ahead of the cows to open the barn door for them.

I knew they were right behind me, anxious to reach the milking stall where their portion of morning grain waited. They also wished to find relief from the heavy load of milk that swelled their udders and slowed their walk.

I began my whistling again. A bird joined me, off to the right, and I turned my head to look for it. It was high in a poplar tree by the hen house, and by its vigorous song I imagined that it was just as happy with the early morning as I was.

From somewhere in Turleys' pasture a cow bawled and another answered. Perhaps a mother had become separated from her baby and was calling it for breakfast.

I opened the barn door for the cows and turned right back to the house for the milk pails. I knew the three cows would find their own way to their stalls and be appreciatively feeding on the chop when I returned. I could have gone the entire milking time without fastening the bars that held them in position, but I never did. I knew they wouldn't move from their places, heads between the stanchion bars, bodies motionless except for the ever-flicking tails and an occasional shift of a foot; but when I returned with the milk pails I fastened the bars just as I always had. It was pure habit I guess—but it was the way Grandpa had taught me.

The jersey gazed back at me with soft brown eyes as I hooked a toe under the milking stool and pulled it up to her side.

"What's the matter?" I chuckled. "You think I'm too lazy to bend over?"

I rubbed her side and eased myself onto the stool beside her, then reached out to brush off her taut bag, wash it a bit, and gently start the flow of milk.

"Well, maybe I am," I conceded. "But a fella has to conserve all the energy he can. I've a busy day ahead. I start plantin' today.

Just as soon as I get the chores done. My own fields. Never planted 'my own fields' before."

I grinned and began the steady stream of milk that would soon fill the pail with rich, warm, foamy liquid.

I would never have been able to explain to anyone why I talked to the cow. I mean, no one would understand if they hadn't spent time in a barn at 5:00 in the morning doing the milking.

A barn cat, meowing, brushed itself against my pant leg. I didn't know if the soft sound was my welcome or an urge for me to hurry. I stopped long enough to squirt some milk in the cat's direction. It immediately sat back on its haunches, front paws batting in the air as though to capture every drop of milk and direct it toward its open mouth.

We were rather good at this—the gray tom and I. But then, we'd had a few years of practice. He sat there guzzling contentedly as I gave him squirt after squirt.

"Go on, now," I said at last. "I've got chores to do. You'll get your fill as soon as I'm done here."

The cat seemed to understand. He walked off a few feet and sat down to begin carefully grooming his spattered face.

The milking didn't take long, so after giving each cow a final pat on the flank, I left them, and carried two brimming pails of milk to the house. I would need to return for the third one, which was now hanging on a peg beyond the reach of the barn cats.

In spite of the early hour, Mary was moving briskly about the kitchen when I entered with the milk. I thought I noticed a certain gleam in her eyes—but perhaps it was just fanciful on my part. The fact that I was feeling so good seemed to be affecting my whole outlook on life.

Pixie was there too, rubbing against my legs, looking for

her share of attention. I reached down and scratched her soft, silky ear. She was no longer the puppy I had learned to love. The years had passed by and Pixie was now old in dog years. She had remained behind, curled and contented, when I'd left my bed that morning. And I had been happy to let her sleep on. I rubbed her soft side and she licked at my hand.

"Mornin', Josh," Mary said cheerily. And without even waiting for my reply she went on, "My, you're up early. Don't know how you can even see out there in the barn."

"I waited for some light," I answered with a smile. "At least it was gettin' light when I went out." Then I added, "True, the barn stays dark a bit longer than the outside world, but I know my way around out there well enough that I don't need much light."

Mary smiled, adding to the brightness of the morning.

"Do you want to eat early?" she asked.

"I still have some chores to do."

Mary's eyes lifted to the kitchen clock, and mine followed.

"Guess I will be ready before the rest of them," I admitted. "Want to start plantin' just as soon as I can."

"I'll git your breakfast," Mary said simply and moved toward the pantry.

"Thanks. I—I hate for you to get breakfast twice, but I'm kind of anxious—"

I needn't have tried to explain. As Mary tied her apron around her slim waist, without even turning to look at me she answered, "In plantin' and harvest time, a man doesn't want to lose any time gittin' to his fields. An early breakfast is no problem—an' we sure don't need to be wakin' the rest of the house."

I hadn't missed Mary's reference to "a man" and "his fields," and my heart beat a little faster. Then my thoughts hurried on to Grandpa, rather old and tired out after all his years of farming, then to Uncle Charlie, all crippled up with his arthritis. I wondered sadly just how much sleep he had been able to get over the night hours. My thoughts went on to Matilda. She was testing her pupils again at the nearby schoolhouse, and I knew she had been staying up late marking papers for a number of nights in a row. I nodded my head in agreement with Mary's simple statement. They all needed their sleep, all right.

"I'll only be another half hour or so," I reported to Mary and then went to strain the milk into the bowl of the cream separator.

"You go on," Mary prompted. "I'll tend to that."

My eyes questioned her, though it was true that Mary had often stepped forward to help with such tasks in the past.

Her eyes held mine steadily, and I knew she wished to take over the chore.

"At least let me strain it," I urged. "These pails are heavy to lift."

Mary did not argue with that. Her eyes followed the stream of milk from the pail into the large bowl of the separator.

"The jersey's?" she asked me. But she didn't wait for my reply. "My, such rich milk. I think I'll separate it by itself and keep the cream aside. Just think of the butter it'll make!"

I could hear the smile in Mary's voice even though I was too busy to look at her face.

I positioned the pail under the separator for Mary and turned to go back to the other chores. On my way to the barn to pick up the remaining pail of milk, I stopped by the tractor and ran a hand over its still-shiny fender. I could hardly wait to crawl up into the seat and begin passing back and forth over my fields, dropping the seed that would mean a bountiful harvest. I lifted my eyes toward heaven, and an unspoken prayer of thanks welled up within me. I'm not sure, but there could have been a few tears in my eyes.

I turned back to the chores at hand. I was whistling a tune I had learned some time back in my childhood, a tune I had sung frequently over the years. But it swelled in my heart in a new way now: "Praise God from whom all blessings flow. . . ."

Chapter 2

Togetherness

I WAS TIRED AND stiff when I climbed down from the tractor that evening. Already the sun was disappearing in the western sky and there was a slight chill in the air. It was, after all, still early spring. I had been riding the tractor almost constantly since sunup. Mary had brought my noon meal and an afternoon snack to the field to save me time. I was glad I wasn't driving a team that would need to stop for a rest and nourishment. The tractor didn't complain about the long hours, though I did need to stop to refuel now and then.

I was a bit surprised at the aches and pains in my back and legs. But then I remembered I'd been bouncing and jostling my way over the field for several hours, and it always took a few days for my body to readjust.

I moved toward the smell of roast beef, my feet reluctant to proceed as quickly as my stomach was demanding. I hadn't realized just how hungry I was until I smelled supper in the air.

"Are you finally stopping for the night?" Matilda good-naturedly asked.

I tried to disguise my stiffness as I stepped up onto the back porch. Matilda was seated on the porch swing, a cup of tea in her hands.

"I was beginning to think we'd never eat," she continued. "This is all Mary would let me have to tide me over till supper."

I stopped mid-stride. "Why?" I asked, surprised. Mary wasn't one to withhold victuals from anybody.

"Well," laughed Matilda. "Guess I'm exaggerating some. Truth is, Mary would have let us go ahead, but we all opted to wait for you."

"I'm sorry—" I began. "If I'd known—"

But Matilda interrupted me. "We all know how important it is to get the crop in. We didn't mind waiting." She stood to her feet and took another dainty sip of the tea, then looked at me, her eyes sparkling. "Honest!" she said frankly, and I believed her.

I held the kitchen door for Matilda and followed right behind into the aroma-filled room. Grandpa was reading a paper in his favorite chair by the window. Uncle Charlie sat on the couch along the west wall gently massaging his gnarled hands, and I knew without asking that they were paining him again. As soon as he felt my eyes on him, he stopped the rubbing and let the hands drop idly into his lap.

Mary was at the big kitchen stove spooning food into serving bowls. She turned, glanced over her shoulder and gave me a smile. I thought she would ask a question, but she didn't—at least not vocally. Maybe her eyes found their answer, I don't know, but she smiled softly again and turned back to the stove.

"We're ready as soon as you wash, Josh," she said.

I crossed to the corner sink with its big farm basin and

noticed that it had already been filled with warm water. I didn't know who had thoughtfully supplied the water, but I did think, with appreciation, that I sure was well looked after.

It didn't take long to scrub my face and hands clean enough to appear at the supper table. By the time I'd re-hung the towel, the rest of the family had gathered around the table. I took my place beside them and bowed as Grandpa asked the grace.

When we lifted our heads and began to help ourselves from Mary's heaping bowls, Grandpa spoke for the first time.

"How'd it go, Boy?"

He still called me "Boy." Guess to Grandpa I would always be Boy no matter how old I grew or whether I was a farm owner or not. I didn't mind. It made me feel "belongin'."

"Good," I replied around a mouthful of fresh bread.

"Tractor workin' right?"

I nodded, my mouth too full to venture an answer.

Uncle Charlie took a long draft of his coffee. "Thet there noise must nigh burst yer eardrums," he ventured. "Think I'd rather drive me a team."

I grinned. Uncle Charlie had a bit of a hard time adjusting to farm machinery that didn't require four-footed horsepower.

I swallowed sufficiently to make a decent reply. "It's noisier but faster, and one needn't stop for restin' or feedin' either."

Uncle Charlie chuckled a bit. "I had my eye on the field, Josh," he reminded me, "and seems to me I saw ya stop different times today to feed thet critter's iron belly."

I laughed along with Uncle Charlie. He'd made his point.

"I think I'd like to drive a tractor," put in Matilda, and I chuckled again at the picture that little bit of a woman would make up there on the seat of the big tractor.

Matilda must have misread my laughter, for her chin went up

stubbornly. "I could, you know," she argued. "Bet I could. All you have to do is to put your foot on that—that thing, and move that lever now and then and turn the wheel where you want it to go."

Even Grandpa was chuckling now.

Matilda looked to Mary. "We could—couldn't we, Mary?" she challenged.

Mary fidgeted slightly. "I—I don't really know, but I—I think I'd just as soon leave the tractor to Josh."

Her eyes met mine for an instance. I noticed the slight color flush her cheeks before she lowered her head. For some silly reason I couldn't have explained, I felt that I had just been given a compliment. Mary often affected me that way—with just a look or a word she could make me feel like a man—a man in charge and capable. I felt my own cheeks warm slightly.

"Someday—" began Matilda, and I looked at her, waiting for her to go on. I was hoping to be able to tease her good-naturedly just a bit; but she would not meet my eyes, and she let the rest of her comment go unsaid.

Supper finished up with Mary's bread pudding, one of my favorite desserts. There was thick whipped cream for the topping, and I was sure this was how some of the jersey's cream had been used.

After enjoying a man-sized portion, I reluctantly pushed back from the table and got slowly to my feet. Uncle Charlie moved at the same time, and I knew he was getting set to give Mary a hand with the dishes.

"I can help tonight, Uncle Charlie," Matilda spoke up.

Now there was nothing new about Matilda calling him Uncle Charlie. Both she and Mary called him such, just like they did when talking to my grandfather. It seemed to please everyone all around. Guess we felt more like family than employer and employee and boarder. What had caught my attention was Matilda's offer. Not that Matilda didn't often help Mary with her household chores, but lately Matilda had been too busy to do anything but correct papers and prepare lessons.

"What happened to the classroom work?" I asked her.

"All done. Finally! And believe me, I feel like celebrating."

Matilda swirled around, her long, full skirt flowing out around her. In one hand she held the sugar bowl and in the other the cream pitcher.

Uncle Charlie looked at her with a twinkle in his eyes. "Seems like ya oughta find a better way to celebrate than with the cream and sugar," he teased.

"Well, Josh is always too busy to celebrate," Matilda teased back, pretending to pout. And she looked deliberately at me and exaggeratedly fluttered her long, dark eyelashes.

Laughter filled the kitchen. Matilda was always bringing laughter with her lighthearted teasing, but for some reason this time her teasing did not have me laughing. It gave me a funny feeling way down deep inside, and I moved for the peg where my farm jacket hung beside the door.

"Where ya goin'?" asked Uncle Charlie, and when I turned to look at him I caught his wink directed at Matilda. "Gonna feed thet there tractor agin?"

"I've got chores," I answered as evenly as I could.

"The chores be all done, Boy," cut in Grandpa.

I stood, my outreached hand dumbly dangling the jacket, my eyes moving from face to face in the kitchen. They all seemed to be in a jovial mood, and I wasn't quite sure if they were serious or funnin' me. It was to Mary that I looked for the final answer. She just nodded her head in agreement.

"All of them?" I had to ask.

"All of 'em," said Grandpa.

For a moment I wanted to protest. It was my farm. I could do my own chores. But then I quickly realized how foolish that was—and how tired I was—and my hand relinquished my coat to the peg again. I turned and smiled at the household of people.

"Thanks," I said simply and gave my shoulders a slight shrug. "Thanks to whoever did them."

"We all pitched in," replied Grandpa. "Little here, a little there and had 'em done in no time."

"Thanks," I said again.

"So you see," teased Matilda, fluttering her eyelashes again, "you will have time to help celebrate."

I was ready for the challenge now. "Okay," I answered, "checkers—right after dishes." And I reached for a tea towel and stepped up beside Mary. "I'll dry—you put things away," I dared order Matilda.

"Checkers?" Matilda commented. "Not exactly a corn roast or a pie social—but I guess it'll have to do," and to the accompaniment of chuckles from the two older men, she moved quickly to put away the dishes as I dried them.

When the last plate was on the shelf, Matilda and I turned to the checkerboard, and Mary picked up some handwork that always seemed to appear when she had what she called a "free moment." Grandpa and Uncle Charlie spent a little more time poring over newspapers. I wasn't sure if we had received a new one or if they were just rereading an old one, but I didn't ask. Beside us on the bureau squawked the raspy radio. I enjoyed the soft music but paid little attention to the commentary that interrupted it at intervals.

It wasn't too hard for me to beat Matilda at checkers. She had a keen mind and could have offered some real serious competition if she hadn't been so impatient. As it was, she played more for the fun than for the challenge, and for three games in a row I turned out the victor.

At the end of the third game I stood and stretched.

"Is that enough 'celebratin' for one evening?" I teased Matilda.

"It'll do," she answered with a flip of her head that made her pinned-up curls bounce. "But next time I'll insist on lawn croquet."

Matilda was an expert at lawn croquet. In fact, whenever there was a matchup, I always hoped Matilda would be my partner. Now I just smiled and tried to stifle a yawn.

Mary laid aside her handwork. "Would you like something to eat or drink before bedtime, Josh?" she asked me and started to leave her chair for the cupboard.

"No, thanks. It's been a long day. I think I'll just go on up to bed." As soon as I said the words, I realized the day had been equally long for Mary. "You must be tired, too," I said, studying her face. "You've been up 'most as long as I have."

Mary brushed the remark aside and went to put on a pot of coffee for Grandpa and Uncle Charlie.

There was the rustle of paper as Grandpa put down what he was reading and took off his glasses.

"I'm plannin' to go on into town tomorrow, Josh," he said, folding up his glasses and placing them on the bureau beside the sputtering radio. "Anything you be needin'?"

I tried to think but my head was a bit foggy. I finally shook it. "If I think of anything I'll leave a note on the table," I promised. "Can't think of anything now."

"You got a list, Mary?" went on Grandpa. "Or would ya rather come on along and do yer own choosin'?"

I stood long enough to watch Mary slowly shake her head. "It takes too much time to ride on in and back," she said. "I'll just send a list."

I took three steps toward the stairway and then turned. "I've been thinkin'," I said, half teasingly but with a hint of seriousness, "maybe when we get in this year's crop, we oughta get us one of those motor cars. We could be in town and back before ya know it."

I don't know just what I expected, but I sure did get a reaction. Grandpa raised his shaggy eyebrows and studied me to see if I was serious. Uncle Charlie stopped rubbing his gnarly fingers and stared open-mouthed. And Mary stopped right in her tracks, one hand reaching out to set the coffeepot on the kitchen stove. But Matilda's response was vocal. "Yes!" she exclaimed, just like that, and she clapped her hands and ran to me. "Oh, yes, Josh!" she said again, her cheeks flushed and her eyes shining. "Get one, Josh. Get one." And she reached out impulsively and gave me a quick hug that almost knocked me off balance.

"Whoa-a," I said, disengaging myself from her arms. "I said 'maybe'—after the crop is off. I'm just plantin' it, remember? We've got a long time to wait."

Matilda stepped back, her eyes still shining. She clapped her hands again, not the least bit daunted. "Now, that's what I call really celebrating, Josh," she enthused, her hands clasped together in front of her.

I let my eyes travel back over the room. Mary had finally set down the coffeepot. Uncle Charlie had closed his mouth and was chewing on a corner of his mustache, and Grandpa's eyebrows were back where they belonged.

I shrugged my shoulders carelessly. "It's just something to be thinkin' on," I repeated lamely and headed for the stairs and my bed.

Chapter 3

Visitors

THE SPRING PLANTING WENT steadily forward. The tractor chugged on with only minor adjustments and repairs. The family continued to help with evening chores and work about the farmyard. Only one rain slowed me down and then it was just a few days—enough for me to sort of catch my breath and do a few little extras that always seem to need doing around a farm.

Matilda never gave me a moment's peace about the motor car. I began to wish I hadn't mentioned it. Still, her enthusiastic arguments in favor of the vehicle may have gone a long way toward influencing Grandpa and Uncle Charlie. At any rate, I never did hear much opposition to the idea, and everybody seemed to be holding their breath—waiting to see what the harvest would bring.

About the same time I finished the planting, the school doors closed for another year and Matilda left for her home again.

"Oh, Josh," she enthused on before departing, "I can hardly wait for fall—and the car. It'll be such fun, Josh!" She emitted a strange little sound like a combination sigh and groan.

"I haven't promised," I reminded her. "Just said I'd be thinkin' on it."

"I know. I know. And it will be such fun!" Apparently Matilda didn't want to hear of the possibility of *not* getting a car, so I let the matter drop.

As usual, Matilda and Mary's goodbye was rather emotional. They had grown to be like sisters in their affection and missed each other during the summer months.

"Oh, I'll be lonely without her," Mary half-whispered after Matilda was gone, and she slyly wiped her cheek with her handkerchief.

"Summer will pass quickly," I tried to console her.

"The house is always so—so *quiet* when she's gone," she responded.

It is quiet without Matilda's bubbly enthusiasm, I mentally agreed.

"You'll be busy with the garden," I reminded Mary.

She nodded; then after a moment of silence she said wistfully, "Maybe Lou will let Sarah Jane come visit for a while. She is 'most as chattery as Matilda."

I smiled at the thought. Sarah Jane was getting to be quite a little lady. And it was true that she was "chattery."

"Maybe," I responded, "for a few days. Lou counts on Sarah for running errands and entertaining her two little brothers."

Mary thoughtfully spoke as though to herself. "Lou does need her more than I do. It was selfish of me to—"

But I interrupted. "It wasn't selfish. Grandpa and Uncle Charlie—and me—we all look forward to her coming."

"Maybe we could have Jon come to the farm, too," Mary brightened. "That would leave Lou with just the baby."

I wasn't sure Mary wanted to take on the lively Jon plus all of the household and garden chores of farm life. I was about to say so, but she placed a hand on my arm, seeming to know just what I was thinking.

"It wouldn't be so bad," she argued. "Sarah would help with Jon, and there is lots for a boy to do on the farm, and the garden isn't ready for pickin' or cannin' yet, and he's usually not *too* rascally." She looked a bit doubtful about her last statement. "Besides," she hurried on, "it sure would make the house more—more—"

I looked at the small hand resting on my arm. It was hard for me to argue against Mary, but I did wonder if she was thinking straight to figure that Jon wouldn't take much time or trouble.

"It would help the summer pass more quickly," she finished lamely.

"Why don't you try it for a few days—to start with? Make sure you aren't gettin' in over your head," I advised.

Mary smiled, and I knew she was pleased with my qualified consent.

It wasn't that Jon was a bad boy, and it certainly wasn't that I didn't love my young nephew, but he was one of the busiest and most curious children I had ever known. His poking and prodding into things invariably got him into some kind of trouble.

"Keep him away from the tractor," I added quite firmly, remembering the time Jon had poured dirt in the gas tank.

Mary just nodded. "I'll check with Lou next time I'm in town," she promised. I couldn't help but think that a break from Sarah and Jon might be a welcome change for my Aunt Lou.

True to her word, Mary made arrangements with Lou. And before the week was out, Sarah and Jon had joined us at the farm. Sarah busied herself with copying the activities of Mary. She helped bake bread, churn butter and wash clothes. She even spent time in the garden pulling weeds—along with a few carrots and turnips—and washed dishes, very slowly, doing more playing in the soapy water than scrubbing the plates and cups. But Sarah seemed to fit very nicely into the farm life, and we all enjoyed her chatter and sunny disposition.

Grandpa and Uncle Charlie tried their best to keep young Jon entertained. They whittled him whistles and slingshots, fashioned him fish poles and found him a barn kitten. But, still, Jon seemed to be continually slipping out from under supervision, off finding entertainment of his own making.

In the few days he was with us he got into more scrapes and mischief—not out of naughtiness but "just tryin' to he'p." He dumped all the hens' water and filled their drinking dishes with hay—he said they looked hungry. He tied the farm dog to a tree with so many knots that it took Grandpa most of an afternoon to get him released again—he said he was afraid "Fritz might get runned over by the tractor." He shot a rock through the front room window with the slingshot he was not to play with around the house—he said that it "went off" when he wasn't ready. He picked a whole pail of tiny apples that were just beginning to form nicely on the apple trees—he wanted to help Mary with an apple pie. He visited the hen house and threw a couple dozen eggs at the old sow who fed in the nearby pen—he wanted to teach her a trick, "like Pixie," of snatching food from the air.

And, as far as I was concerned, the worst stunt of all was helping himself to a bottle of India ink from Matilda's supply desk and sneaking up on unsuspecting Chester, climbing the corral fence and pouring it all over the horse's back. He wanted to "surprise Unc'a Josh" with a pretty, spotted horse like one he had seen in a picture book.

We had a family council that night. I was ready to send Jon on home, but Mary argued that he really wasn't naughty and needed a chance to learn about the farm. Grandpa sided with her. How could the boy learn what he could and couldn't do if he wasn't given the chance to do a little exploring? So Jon stayed on, but we gave the four-year-old more rules and tried to watch him even closer.

I was busy repairing the back pasture fence when Jon joined me one afternoon.

"Hi, Unc'a Josh," he greeted me warmly. I looked at the bright eyes and mop of brown hair.

"Hi, fella," I responded a bit cautiously. "Does Mary know you're here?"

Jon did not answer my question but held a little red pail as high as his short arm could hoist it.

"Brought ya a drink," he announced. "Are ya thirsty?"

The summer sun was hot, and I *was* thirsty. I stopped to wipe the sweat from my brow and reached for the pail the boy held out to me.

"Auntie Mary said ya would be thirsty," Jon continued. Lou had her children refer to Mary as "auntie" as a term of respect.

My eyes shifted to the nearby farmhouse. I was close enough that I didn't need to be waited on—I could walk to the house or the well for a drink. Still, maybe Mary thought a bit of a stroll and an "errand" would do the small boy good. I sat down on the grass and pulled Jon onto my knee, one hand supporting the pail.

"Where's Mary?" I asked him, looking at the dirt streaks on his hands and face.

"Busy doin' some'pin," he answered.

"So you brought me a drink?"

He nodded.

"That was mighty nice," I complimented Jon. "Thank you."

I lifted the pail to my lips. The water was not as cool as usually comes from our deep well, and I couldn't help but wonder just how long Jon had been on his journey. At least it was wet. I took another long drink.

"So what have you been doing today?" I asked Jon.

He thought about that for a few moments before answering.

"I he'ped Grandpa hoe the garden," he said brightly and then added more soberly, "but he said, 'Thet's enough, Jonathan,' and sent me back to Auntie Mary."

I tousled his hair. "And why did he do that?" I questioned. "Did you mix up weeds and vegetables?"

Jon nodded his head, his eyes thoughtful. "I guess it was peas," he said somberly, and I had to hide my smile.

"Then I brought in the clothes for Auntie Mary," he began, but ended with a shrug of his small shoulders. "But she hada take 'em back agin. They wasn't dry yet." Then Jon added quickly as though with great relief, "But Auntie Mary din't scold me. Jest took the clothes and hung some back up an'—" His eyes lowered and then lifted again to mine. He finished with a grin that told me everything was all right. "An' washed some of 'em agin an' then hung *them* back up, too."

Poor Mary. She had enough work without re-doing the wash.

"Here comes Aunt Mary now!" Jon excitedly pointed toward the farm buildings.

He was right. Mary and Sarah were coming our way.

"We brought you something, Uncle Josh," Sarah called before they reached us.

I looked at the small container in Sarah's hands and then to Mary. Both young ladies seemed pleased with themselves.

"Do I have to guess?" I asked Sarah.

Puffing, she reached the spot where Jon and I still sat on the ground.

"It's a drink," she said proudly.

"A drink? That's nice. But Jon here"—I ruffled the boy's hair again—"he already beat you to it. But I guess another drink would—"

But I stopped. The mention of the drink brought to me by young Jon had made Mary's face blanch, her hand went to her mouth and she stood staring down at the red pail.

"Is something wrong?" I asked Mary, but it was Sarah who answered the question for me, though in a rather roundabout fashion.

"In that?" she squealed, pointing her finger at the red pail in the grass. Before I could even answer her she went on, "Jon was botherin' Grandpa in the garden—hoeing up things—so Grandpa gave him that pail and sent him to water the flowers."

That didn't sound so bad. I didn't mind sharing water with the flowers. But Mary's face was still pale and she hadn't said one word except for a gaspy little, "Oh, Joshua."

"But," went on Sarah, "Jon was dipping water from the stock trough!"

For a moment my stomach rebelled. I even thought I might

be sick. The thought of the horses and cattle slurping and snorting in my drinking water made my insides heave. I looked up at Mary's white face and agonized expression. And then the whole thing struck me funny, and I pulled Jon closer into my arms, rolled over in the grass and began to tickle him and laugh. Not just little chuckles, but outright guffaws. Mary's color returned to normal, and I saw she was trying to hide a snicker behind her hand. Then she looked at Jon and me tumbling on the grass together and began to laugh right along with me. Now my stomach hurt from laughter.

When we finally got ourselves under control, we all sat down on the ground together and shared the cool lemonade Mary and Sarah had brought.

"I guess if I can drink with the cows and horses, I can use the same cup as family," I said and began to laugh again.

"We have cookies, too," Sarah informed me importantly. I think she was trying to get me to settle down. She didn't seem to understand why I thought my drink from the stock trough was so funny. I tried to respond properly to Sarah's announcement.

"Cookies? What kind? Where did you find cookies?"

"They're sugar cookies and I made 'em—myself." And then she quickly corrected her statement. "Auntie Mary and me made 'em."

"Can I have one? Can I have one, Sarah?" Jon was asking. Sure enough, there were some for all of us.

I guess the lemonade and the sugar cookies had a settling effect on my stomach. At any rate, I suffered no ill effects from drinking water out of the stock trough, though I did determine that in the future I would carefully check any food or drink offered me from the hand of my young nephew.

Chapter 4

Summer

THINGS SETTLED DOWN AGAIN after Sarah and Jon went off to their home. I think even Mary was glad for the peace and quiet, though she never admitted it. She had much to do, with the garden now in full swing. Her hands never seemed to be empty nor her body still.

The summer was busy for me as well. There was haying, the war with farm weeds, the continual care of the stock and fences; and before we could scarcely turn around, the summer would be drawing to an end.

I was glad for Sundays. It was the one day of the week that, with a clear conscience and no guilty feelings, one could actually take a bit of a break. It was good to be driving into town for the church service—though I must confess that as I sat behind the slow-moving team, I kept thinking more and more of the time we'd save in traveling if I had that motor car.

On a couple of Sundays we stayed on to dinner with Lou and

Nat and their three. That was about the only chance we really had to catch up on the happenings of one another's lives.

Baby Timothy was growing so fast it was hard to keep up to him. He celebrated his first birthday in June and was busy with the task of learning how to walk—how to run might more aptly describe it. Timmy wanted to be in on the fun with his older brother and sister and tagged around after them as fast as his sturdy little legs would allow.

"The crop's looking good and seems to be a little ahead of schedule," I told Nat over one of our Sunday dinners. "It might well be our best crop yet," I admitted.

But I went from day to day with one eye on the sky and the other on my fields. I knew without being told that one good hailstorm could change everything, and deep inside me, I kind of wished there was some way I could make a little bargain with God. But of course I didn't try. I had the good sense—and faith—to know that He knew all about our needs and my wishes, and that in His love He would take care of our future. But oh, my, how I did hope that the future didn't include hail.

In next to no time Matilda was breezing in again. The two girls hugged and squealed and laughed like they'd been apart for years. Even Grandpa and Uncle Charlie got enthusiastic squeezes. I accepted a small hug myself, then backed up and looked at Matilda's glowing face.

"How's the crop, Josh?" she burst out before I had a chance to open my mouth. No "How are you?" or anything like that, but "How's the crop?" and I knew just what she was thinking about. I was prepared to tease her a bit.

I shrugged my shoulders and put a glum look on my face. "It might pay for the cuttin'," I informed her drearily. "That is, if we don't get any hail or such."

Matilda's mouth went down at the corners, and a sound of disappointment escaped her lips.

"Look on the bright side," I said, patting her shoulder. "With good weather and no more problems, we'll have a bit of seed grain for next spring."

Matilda looked awfully disappointed, even shamefaced.

"I told all my friends that you'd be getting a—a motor car," she said softly, her voice catching on the last word.

"Well, now, I didn't make me any promises on that, did I?" I said, keeping my expression somber. "Maybe you shouldn't'a been tellin' tales out of school." But when she looked like she might cry, I decided I had gone far enough.

"I'm just joshin'," I grinned at her. "The crop looks good. Real good." And as Matilda was about to exuberantly throw herself at me I hastened on, "Now remember, I'm still not promisin'. Just been thinkin' on that automobile. No promises."

But Matilda didn't seem one bit worried about the results of "thinkin' on it." Guess she knew me well enough to know I wanted that motor car too.

She punched me on the arm with a little fist, but her eyes were shining. "Oh, Josh," she scolded, "you're mean!"

Grandpa chuckled, and Uncle Charlie just grinned.

When the school year started again, it was rather a traumatic time for Aunt Lou. Sarah Jane started off to first grade. I hadn't realized how tough it was on mothers to see their first baby go off into a whole new world. Lou wanted to be enthusiastic for Sarah's sake, but I knew that if it had been in Lou's power to turn back the clock a year or two, she could not have refrained from doing so.

Mary went into the final stages of putting up summer fruits and vegetables. As I watched the stacks of canning jars fill and refill the kitchen counter top, I wondered how in the world the five of us could ever consume so much food. Part of the answer came when I saw Mary and Grandpa load a whole bunch into the buggy and send it off to town to Aunt Lou. Lou was too busy with her little family and being a pastor's wife to do much canning of her own, Mary reasoned. Lou was deeply appreciative. After all, a pastor's salary didn't leave much room for extras, though I'd never heard Lou complain.

I began to find little pamphlets and newspaper advertisements scattered about the kitchen telling about this motor car or that automobile and the merits of each. I didn't have to guess who was leaving them about, but I did wonder how Matilda was collecting them.

I read the descriptions—just like she knew I would. In fact, I sneaked them off to my own bedroom and lay in bed going over and over them. My, some of them were fancy! I hadn't known that such features existed. Why, you could start the motor without cranking it in the front! Then I would look at the listed price. I hadn't known that they cost so much, either, and doubts began to form in my mind. The same number of dollars could do so many things for the farm. I began to realize that Matilda's little campaign might well come to nothing. It could be sheer foolishness for me to buy a car.

I went into harvest with my mind debating back and forth. One day I would think for sure that I "deserved a car." The whole family deserved a car after all the years of slow team travel. *And think of how much valuable time we'd save,* I'd reason. Then the next day I would think of the farm needs, of the church needs, of my promise to support Camellia in her missionary service, of the stock I could purchase or the things for Mary's kitchen; and I would mentally strike the motor car from my list. Back and forth, this way and that way I argued with myself. Even all of the praying I did about it didn't put my mind at rest.

It did turn out to be a good crop. Even better than I'd dared hope. I watched the bins fill to overflowing with wonderfully healthy grain. I had to purchase an extra bin from the Sanders and pull it into our yard with the tractor. I filled it, too. The good quality grain brought good prices as well. God had truly blessed us.

Now, how did He want me to spend what He had given? How could I be a responsible steward?

I was still busy with the farm duties during the day, but in the evenings I spent hours and hours poring over the account books. I figured this way, then that way. With every load of grain I took to town, the numbers in my little book swelled. There would be a surplus. But would there be enough for the motor car? And if so, was a motor car necessary? Practical? The right thing for the Jones family?

I knew everyone was waiting for my decision. Grandpa and Uncle Charlie did not question me. Mary never made mention of the vehicle, but I could sense that she was sharing my struggle over the decision. Matilda stopped cajoling me about it, but her eyes continually questioned, and I knew she was getting very impatient waiting for me to make up my mind.

I went to my room one night and took out all the advertisements again. I laid aside the one showing the shiny gray Bentley. It was far too fancy and costly for me, though I did allow myself one fleeting mental picture of me purring down our country road at the wheel. I laid aside a few more as well. As the pile of discarded pamphlets grew, a bit of the pride and envy of Joshua Jones was also cast aside. At last I was left with a plain, simple car made by the Ford company. There was plenty of money for the Ford—with a good deal left for other things we needed. I would get the Ford. My conscience could live with that.

I breathed a sigh of relief, laid aside the pamphlet and blew out my light. In the darkness of my room I knelt by my bed to pray. With the decision finally made with the seeming approval of my Father, I welcomed a sense of peace. I slept that night like I hadn't slept in weeks.

The next morning at the breakfast table I cleared my throat to get the family's attention. "I decided to get a car," I announced, and before I could go further there was a squeal from Matilda, a smile from Mary, and a nod from Grandpa. Uncle Charlie just grinned a bit. The long, jarring buggy rides were hard on his arthritic bones.

"Now wait. Now wait," I protested, holding up my hand and directing my words to Matilda. "We can afford a motor car—no problem. But I decided that it won't be a fancy one. No need for that, and it would just set us back. We'll get a simple, practical Ford—none of the gadgets and gizmos."

Matilda sobered.

"But it will have wheels—and get us to where we need to go," I assured them.

Matilda's face brightened again.

"When?" asked Grandpa, and though he tried hard to hide it, I caught the excitement in his voice.

"I'm goin' to town to order it today," I answered, and I had a hard time controlling my own excitement.

Matilda squealed. "Oh, Josh. It's so-o exciting!" she bubbled.

Uncle Charlie's smile widened.

I looked at Mary. Her face was flushed, her eyes shining.

Then she did a most unexpected thing. She reached over and gave my hand a squeeze.

If Matilda had done it, I would have thought nothing of it. In fact, I would have thought nothing of it if Matilda had thrown herself wildly into my arms or flung her arms about my neck and squeezed with all her might—that was just Matilda. But Mary? That quiet little gesture of shared excitement somehow set my pulse to racing.

I flushed slightly as I pulled my eyes back to the other members at the breakfast table and rose slowly to my feet. It was a moment before I found my thoughts, my tongue.

"I—I'll order it—today, but—but I have no idea how long it might be before it comes."

Matilda brought things back to normal. "Oh, I hope it arrives *soon*!" she exclaimed, bouncing up from her chair. "I hope it hurries. We don't have much time. We need it before winter so we can learn to drive it before the snow—"

Matilda caught herself and stopped mid-sentence. Her eyes met mine and she looked like a small child coaxing for a treat. She had been using a lot of "we's," which was rather presumptuous on her part, but I just smiled and gave her a quick wink. I understood.

After we shared our morning devotions together around the breakfast table, I went back to my room and folded the Ford pamphlet and slipped it into my pocket. As soon as I had finished the last of the morning chores, I would saddle Chester and head for town.

Chapter 5

The Ford

LIKE MATILDA, I WAS hoping the car would arrive before snowfall. I wanted the chance to learn to drive it while the roads were still clear.

I managed to keep myself busy with no problem. I must admit I made a few more trips to town than normal. I pretended that I needed things or wanted the mail, but in fact I stopped in to check—with regularity—if there had been any word on the car.

On one such trip to town I found a long, newsy letter from Camellia. She had received word from the Mission Society that she would be leaving for Africa in the spring. She was so excited that her penmanship, usually in character—neat and attractive—was rushed and almost sloppy. This letter conveyed intense excitement.

"I can't believe it, Josh!" she wrote. "After all these years I am finally going to Willie's Africa. To the people he learned to love so. I will be stationed near enough to the village where

Willie served that the mission has promised a trip to the grave site. I will be able to see the spot where Willie's body is lying. I know that it might not seem like much to others, but I think you will understand. I want to personally be able to lay some flowers on Willie's grave. And it will be very special for me to be able to kneel there and ask God to help me in carrying on Willie's ministry.

"I won't be staying in the area. At least not for now. They say it is much too primitive to leave a woman all alone, and there is no other young lady available to live and work with me at present. But I am praying that if it is God's will, He will provide me with a working companion so that we might be able to live there before too long and have a chance to reach Willie's people.

"He used to write me all about them. I can almost see them. There was the chief—a small man by our standards—but, my, he had power! Willie said that the people didn't question his word for one minute. And there was one old woman—I do hope she is still there. She fed Willie from her own cooking pot, even though there was scarcely enough for her own family. Willie was sure she herself must have gone without food numerous times. And the little children. Willie said they followed along behind him, curious as to what this strange white man was going to do. And then there was Andrew. That was not his African name. That was the name Willie gave to him after he became a Christian. He was Willie's only convert. I can hardly wait to meet Andrew."

Camellia's letter went on, but I couldn't continue reading for the moment. It was some time before my eyes were dry enough to see the words on the page. If I missed Willie this much, I couldn't imagine what the loss was like for Camellia.

Camellia wrote about not wanting to leave her mother all

alone. Then she chided herself. Of course her mother would not be alone—she had the same Lord with her who would be with Camellia on the mission field.

"You've always been such a dear friend, Josh, to both Willie and me. I appreciate your friendship now more than ever. And I can never thank you enough for helping with my support so I can go to Africa as Willie and I had planned. I pray for you daily. May God bless you, Josh, and grant to you the desires of your heart, whatever or whoever that might be."

Camellia had underscored "whoever," and I could picture her face with the teasing gleam in her eyes as I read the little message. I felt an emptiness inside of me. Would there ever be anyone else who would take the place of Camellia in my heart? I pushed the thought aside. Camellia was headed for Africa, and for some reason, still a mystery to me, God had chosen for me to stay on the farm.

I read the last paragraph again. "May God bless you, Josh, and grant to you the desires of your heart, whatever—"

I stopped there. I had come into town to check on the Ford again. As my eyes traveled back over the pages of Camellia's letter, the idea of a motor car paled in comparison.

"Lord," I admitted in a simple prayer, "I've got things a bit out of perspective. We need a car. I've weighed the purchase this way and that way, and for all involved it seems like the right move—but help me, Lord, not to get too wrapped up in it. A car is, after all, just a way to get places. These people—these Africans of Camellia's—they are eternal souls. Brothers. Remind me to spend more time in prayer for them as Camellia goes to minister the gospel to them."

I carefully folded Camellia's letter and tucked it in an inside pocket. I didn't even bother to go on down the street to check on the arrival of the car. It would be here when it was here! Instead I turned Chester toward Lou's. The children would welcome a little visit, and it would be nice to sit and share a cup of coffee with Lou.

When we awakened the next morning the ground was covered with snow. I won't pretend it didn't give me a bit of a start. I had so hoped. But I dismissed the thought. Surely a car could be driven in a few inches of snow.

When Matilda came downstairs, she didn't seem to be able to dismiss the snow quite as easily.

"Oh, no-o," she wailed. "What will we do? What will we *do*, Josh? The snow is already here, but the motor car isn't! Oh-h-h." She crossed to the window, swept back Mary's carefully ironed white ruffled curtain and groaned again. "We'll have to learn to drive it in the snow. It would have been so much easier—"

"Guess there's no problem," I was quick to cut in. "We don't have the car yet anyway."

"But it'll be here just any day now and the snow . . ."

But the snow had all disappeared by noon, and two days later the Ford arrived. I thought I had prepared myself for the role of motor-car owner, but when the news reached me I felt a thrill go all through my body. This was followed by a cold sweat. My hands got sticky and my mouth dry and my knees fairly shook with excitement—and just a little fear.

We hitched up the team, and Grandpa and Uncle Charlie drove with me on into town. I couldn't just ride Chester to pick the car up because I needed to drive it back.

We drove right up to Mr. Hickson's, and I pretended nonchalance as I stepped into his office and said I was there to pick up the car. I had the rest of the payment in my coat pocket, pinned in so I wouldn't accidentally lose it. I began to carefully unpin the coat in order to get at my money, but Mr. Hickson rushed right on by me, calling as he went, "It's this way, Josh, an' she's a beaut! Come on in an' git a look at 'er."

I followed, with Grandpa and Uncle Charlie right on my heels.

She was a beaut all right. Never had I seen so much shiny metal. There she stood, black paint gleaming and window glass sparkling. I slowly sucked in my breath. She was beautiful!

I was quite familiar with the few motor cars on our town streets. Several of them were quite fancy, too, but to me this Ford—this car that was mine—was the nicest of the lot.

I moved forward and ran a hand over the shiny fender. Mr. Hickson opened a door.

"An' look in here," he urged. "See them leather seats. Looka that. Looka that."

I moved to look. Sure enough, leather seats—finest black leather one ever saw. I let out the breath I had seemed to be holding. I heard Uncle Charlie say something to Grandpa and Grandpa answer, "Well, whoo-ee!" and I wheeled to look at them. Both of them were grinning. *Standin' there a gazin' at that car like they've never seen nothin' like it before*, I chuckled to myself.

"Whoo-ee," said Grandpa again, and he lifted a hand to stroke the black leather. Uncle Charlie's mustache was twitching. He reached out one gnarled hand to touch the shining glass of the window. For a moment I wondered if there could ever be anything more exciting in life than this—standing there getting a good look at your first car and brand new at that.

I came back down to earth in time to hear Mr. Hickson

saying, "Just a few things to take care of, an' you can drive her right on out of here."

Mr. Hickson was moving back toward his little office, and I turned to follow, though I was feeling a moment of panic. I could "drive her right on out," said Mr. Hickson. But surely Mr. Hickson knew I had never driven a car before. Surely he wouldn't just put me in it and expect—

"Ya got some 'struction papers with this here new Ford?" Grandpa was asking Mr. Hickson very matter-of-factly, and I knew I should have asked the question.

"Of course. Of course," Mr. Hickson answered, nodding his head vigorously. "Everything thet ya need to know is right in here in the office."

Whew! Maybe I wouldn't embarrass myself after all.

"Joe Hess, down the street, has got him a Ford. Much like this one, only not as new," Mr. Hickson was saying. "He'd be glad to come on over here and take Josh for his first run."

"Thet'd be good. Real good," Grandpa agreed. Then added quickly, "Just till he gets the hang of it. He'll catch on real quick. Been driving thet big ol' tractor now fer quite a spell."

Mr. Hickson nodded his head again. "I'll send Mickey right over fer Joe," and making good on his word he called a young fellow from the back room and sent him on his way.

For some reason the rest of them seemed to have forgotten that I was the buyer. Grandpa and Mr. Hickson were busy making plans without me. But they soon turned back to me when it came time for the final payment to be made. I pulled the money from my pocket and Mr. Hickson counted it out.

"Right," he said. "Just right."

That was no news to me. I had checked the money out carefully—three times—before I left home.

By the time we finished with the paperwork Joe was there. He seemed properly impressed with the new car and walked around and around it, studying each feature, especially those that his older model did not have. He didn't say much, but he grinned and he admired and he ran a hand over the black metal now and then.

We all climbed in for our first spin around town. I sat up front with Joe so I might learn all the procedures for driving. Grandpa and Uncle Charlie settled in the back. It was hard to tell who was the most excited.

Mr. Hickson gave it a good crank, we started off with a bit of a jump, and I heard Grandpa gasp, but then we moved out onto Main Street past all the stores and people.

We made quite an impression, you can be sure of that. Heads turned, people stopped, store owners came out of their shops, curtains fluttered at windows and dogs barked and chased us on down the road.

The farther we went the faster we went. It wasn't long until we were whizzing along. It fairly took the breath out of me, but Joe seemed to know just what he was doing, and he maneuvered the car like it was no problem at all.

When we got out in open country he suggested that I give it a try. I was so nervous that my hands shook, but I crawled behind the steering wheel and did just like Joe had showed me. Well, almost. I let the clutch out a bit too quickly, and the Ford bucked like she'd been spurred. It killed the motor and Joe had to get out and give it a crank again. The next time worked better and soon I was steering down the road like I'd been driving all my life.

By the time we got back to town and dropped Joe off, I was getting pretty good. We decided to wheel around to Nat and

Lou's and show off just a bit. I was hoping Nat would be home. A car like this would sure save a pastor some calling time.

Nat was there all right, and we had to show him everything on the Ford that moved. He studied it over and over again, making contented clicking noises and grinning from ear to ear. I felt my buttons pushing at my shirt front. I felt pretty proud and even more grown up than when the farm was signed over to me.

At last we pulled away from our admirers and headed back out on the street again, Jon howling behind us. He wanted to go too. I had already taken them all for a little spin, but I guess that wasn't good enough for young Jon. He wanted to go wherever the car was going.

When we got back to Hickson's, Grandpa climbed out and went to untie the horses from the hitching rail. Uncle Charlie began to climb out too, maybe a little reluctantly. I guess Grandpa must have sensed it. "Why don't you jest go on home with Josh?" he said. "Don't take two of us to drive this poky ol' team."

Uncle Charlie didn't argue. He settled back on that leather seat and took a big breath of the autumn air. Then he pulled out his pocket watch and sat studying the face of it.

"Okay, Josh," he said, and there was a glint in his eye. "Let's see how long it takes 'er to make the trip to the farm."

I grinned, then nodded. I put the Ford into gear and we started out. Once we cleared the town streets I opened her up a bit more. The breeze fairly whipped in the open windows. Way back at the edge of town we could see Grandpa just turning the team and buggy onto the road for home. Then the dust from our wheels blocked him from view, and Uncle Charlie and I were off.

We didn't try to set any records. I drove as sensibly as I knew how. But even with my caution at the wheel, the trip home took only eleven minutes and thirty-seven seconds. Uncle Charlie chuckled gleefully as he held the watch out for me to see.

We turned into our lane. I could hardly wait to show the girls the new car. Then I looked with dismay at the dust that already clung to her shiny exterior and wished there was some way I could quickly polish her up before the introduction. But I realized that would never work, for already Mary was running to meet us.

Chapter 6

A Caller

I HAD PLENTY OF time to show Mary the car, take her for a ride, and wash and polish all the metal and leather before Grandpa pulled into the yard with the team.

I had learned one lesson on the way home. The feel of the fresh autumn air blowing in the open windows might be invigorating, but on our dusty country roads it was not practical. I decided that from now on when the car was on the move, the windows would be kept up. I said as much to Uncle Charlie as he watched me polish and clean.

After Grandpa had gone off to Mary's kitchen with the groceries she had ordered, I settled the team and went back to shining the car. Reluctant to leave the new Ford, I was finally coaxed into the kitchen for tea and cornbread.

As soon as the kitchen clock told us that school would be letting out, we all climbed into the car and set off to pick up Matilda.

"I can hardly wait to see her face when we pull into the school yard," Mary said warmly.

I drove very slowly. I didn't want to get the car all dusty again before Matilda had a chance to see it. Even so, we got a bit ahead of ourselves according to Uncle Charlie's pocket watch and had to pull to the side of the road just over the hill from the schoolhouse. We didn't want to arrive before Matilda was free to dismiss her students.

At last Uncle Charlie gave us the go-ahead, and I hopped out to give the car a crank while Grandpa pulled and pushed the necessary buttons and levers. Joe had said a man could start the car all by himself, but we weren't sure we had the hang of it yet.

We met some of Matilda's students as we chugged up the last hill to the school yard, so we knew that school was over for the day.

If we had expected Matilda to be excited, we weren't disappointed. As we pulled into the school yard, we saw her appear at the window. She probably wondered what the strange sound was. For a moment she stood as though stunned, her eyes wide and hands over her mouth. At Mary's wild waving, Matilda finally came to her senses. She fairly exploded from the door and took the front steps as though they weren't even there.

"It's here! It's here!" she was screaming as she ran toward us. "Oh, Josh, it's here." I decided not to point out that I was well aware of that fact.

She never even stopped to admire the shiny metal I had just worked so hard to polish. She didn't look at the gleaming glass windows. She never slowed down for a moment, just hurled herself at the door, climbed right over Mary in one swift motion and shuffled to settle herself right between the two of us.

"Show me!" she squealed. "Quickly—show me."

"You can't see much scrunched in here," I said a bit sourly, trying to shove over enough to give Matilda room. "You gotta do most of your lookin' from the outside," and I moved to open my door.

But Matilda was shaking her head so vigorously that her curls were coming unpinned. "No," she wailed, grabbing my hand from the door handle. "Show me how to drive."

Grandpa snorted and Uncle Charlie chuckled. Mary just shrugged her slim shoulders and smiled. I was stunned. I sure wasn't prepared to give Matilda a driving lesson in my new car. I'd barely learned how myself. I stalled for time.

"We've come to take you home," I informed her. "Are you ready to go?"

For a moment she seemed not to understand. She took a few gulps of air and then answered me almost sanely, "No, I have to get my books and clean the blackboards and lock the school."

We all piled out. Mary cleaned the blackboards while Matilda gathered her books. Uncle Charlie and Grandpa studied a map on the wall, but I just wandered around picturing the room as it had been when I was a student there.

In the row over by the windows had sat Avery, then me, then Willie—I could see him yet. His mop of unruly hair spilling over his forehead, his freckles scattered across the tip of his nose, his face screwed up in a frown as he worked on an arithmetic problem.

I turned abruptly and walked from the room. Even yet the memories were too painful.

"I'll wait outside," I said with as steady a voice as I could manage and I closed the schoolhouse door rather firmly on the memories.

It didn't take Matilda long and we all climbed back in the car and started down the country road.

We rearranged our load. Mary climbed in the backseat between Grandpa and Uncle Charlie. It was a bit crowded but they didn't seem to mind. Matilda rode in the front by me. Her eyes did not travel over the polished leather upholstery. Instead, they stayed glued to the steering wheel and the controls, watching every movement I made. I knew Matilda would never let me rest until she had been taught how to drive my car.

However, I was not ready to share the driving with anyone just yet. Not even Matilda.

"Why don't you settle back and enjoy the ride?" I urged her. "Remember, it won't be every day that we come and pick you up from school."

I guess she got the message. She sighed and did sit back. Sort of. Though I could still feel her eyes on my hands.

It wasn't long before I relented and did give Matilda a few driving lessons. We did not venture out on the road, only up and down our long farm lane. She caught on quickly, I must admit. I offered to teach Mary how to drive, too, but she just smiled and said she would just as soon let me do it.

The car was certainly an asset and time saver in driving back and forth to town. We looked forward to the family drive each Sunday. It was a bit crowded, but no one complained.

And then the winter snows came deep enough that the car was no longer practical. I drove it into the shed I had built for it and we started using the team again. Never had the trip to town seemed longer than when we were forced to travel it again by sleigh.

The dog was making an awful commotion one evening, and we all rose from our places to look out the window. We hadn't been expecting any callers. The evening was chilly, but not inhuman. There was no sharp wind blowing and the moon was bright. Still, we couldn't figure out why anyone would be making house calls on horseback at such an hour. I had a momentary pang that something might be wrong in town and Uncle Nat had come to inform us.

But it wasn't Uncle Nat. Relieved, I realized the traveler was a stranger. Well, not exactly a stranger. I had seen him once or twice, and from the greetings later in our kitchen, I came to realize that both Mary and Matilda had met him before.

But when Grandpa had answered his knock and opened the door, he didn't seem to know who the young man was. He extended his hand cordially anyway and offered for the young fella to come in.

"Don't believe I've had the pleasure," Grandpa was saying as he shook the hand firmly, and the man answered cheerily enough, "Sanders. Will Sanders. We bought the place just over yonder," and he nodded his head to the east.

"Sanders," repeated Grandpa. "Thought I'd met Sanders." Grandpa looked a bit perplexed. "Thet weren't yer pa, were it?"

"No, sir. My oldest brother. He bought the place. My pa's been gone for nigh unto seven years now."

"Sorry to hear thet," Grandpa said sincerely. "Come in an' sit ya down. Is there something we can be a helpin' ya with?"

The young man smiled easily. "Thank you, no," he answered evenly. "Just callin'." He made no move toward a chair.

All of this conversation had taken place while the rest of us looked on. I guess Will figured it was time to change all that.

His eyes traveled around the room. He nodded briefly to Uncle Charlie, studied me for a moment and then turned his gaze toward the two girls. That was the first he smiled. He reached to remove his hat and with a slight nod in the girls' direction said, "Hello, Miss Turley, Miss Hopkins."

That was when I began to study the man before me.

A little taller than me, his shoulders were broader, hips slimmer. Even in the lamplight I could see the waves of dark hair and the deep-set dark eyes. His jaw was rather square and his nose straight. When he smiled he showed a row of even, white teeth. Even I was smart enough to know that ladies would consider him a good-looking man. I stirred uneasily as Mary and Matilda acknowledged his greeting. Both of them had a flush on their cheeks and shine to their eyes.

Mary was the first to move forward.

"Won't you come in, Mr. Sanders," she greeted him cordially. "Here, let me have your hat and coat."

Will Sanders passed Mary his hat and took off his heavy winter coat. Mary took both to a peg reserved for visitors' wraps in the corner.

I had never seen Matilda silent for so many minutes before.

"I didn't realize you were staying on," she finally ventured with a shy look in Sander's direction.

"Well, I had thought about going back to the city for the winter, but my brother said he could sure use some help with the choring."

I shifted uneasily again.

"Have you met Josh?" asked Mary, returning from hanging up the man's hat and coat.

The eyes shifted to me. He studied me for a moment before

saying slowly, rather deliberately, "I don't believe I've had the privilege," and he smiled a bit too familiarly, I thought.

I stepped forward and extended my hand. It seemed like the neighborly thing to do. He shook it firmly. I wondered if he was trying to make me cringe under his grip. I found my fingers tightening around his. I wanted the man to know that other men had strength in their hands as well.

For a moment our eyes locked, and I could see in his expression some sort of challenge. I wasn't sure what it was all about, but I sure felt ill at ease.

After just sitting around for a spell thinking up things to talk about like weather and cattle feed, Matilda suggested that we play some Chinese checkers. We moved our chairs into position around the table. The game went well enough. For some reason I can't explain, it was very important to me that I win. I did. But just. Then the next game was won by Mary. That didn't bother me a bit, but it did bother me some that young Sanders came in second.

Mary fixed a little snack, and Grandpa and Uncle Charlie joined us around the table. Matilda carried most of the conversation. She and Sanders chatted on merrily, and occasionally he turned and offered some comment to Mary and she responded. I didn't pay too much attention to it all. I couldn't see where it concerned me much anyway. Then a comment of Matilda's caught my ear.

"Josh has a new Ford, but with the snow so deep he has it put away for now."

I felt my pride swell a bit. Here was one area where I had an edge on the city slicker fella. But his words quickly cut me down to size again.

"I have a silver Bentley, but I left it in the city. I wasn't sure of the country roads, and I didn't want it damaged. I'm thinking of bringing it on out in the spring."

I had a sinking feeling in the pit of my stomach.

Mary said nothing but Matilda swooned. "A silver Bentley! I saw one of those in an advertising pamphlet. They are just gorgeous."

The young man nodded matter-of-factly as though a silver Bentley was really the least of the "gorgeous" things he possessed.

After a lot of small talk, mostly centered on Will Sanders, he finally decided to go. If he expected an argument from me, he sure was mistaken. But as he took his leave, he promised to be back. Not "may I" or "by your leave" or anything like that. Just "I'll drop back again the first chance I get." I cringed inside.

After he'd finally gone I went up to bed as soon as I could tactfully excuse myself. Even with my door closed I could hear Mary and Matilda talking and giggling like a couple of schoolgirls. The whole thing disturbed me so much I could hardly concentrate as I read my nightly Bible passage and tried to pray. Yet I couldn't put into thoughts or words just why I felt as I did. I tried hard to shove the uneasy feelings aside and get to sleep, but it was too big a job for me. I tossed and turned until I heard the clock strike three—still sleep eluded me. I slammed my fist into my pillow and wished fervently that I had never laid eyes on the guy.

CHAPTER 7

Changes

I AWOKE STILL TIRED and grumpy from my lack of sleep. I had never felt quite so disturbed in my entire life, and I couldn't make heads or tails of it. I knew it had something to do with that young whippersnapper Will Sanders, but what he might have done to merit such feelings on my part I had no idea. He seemed like a decent enough chap, and he certainly had behaved himself in gentlemanly fashion while he had been a guest—though an uninvited one—in our home.

No one else seemed to take offense at his sudden appearance, and *some* members of the household actually seemed to favor his visit.

Somehow I knew he had touched on a raw nerve. After pondering the situation, I realized I resented the attention that Matilda and Mary had given to him. I had no reason to resent it, but the feeling was there. I felt challenged—backed up in my own corner. But what was I trying to defend? And why did the presence of the new neighbor put me on the defensive?

I shoved the whole thing aside, for it was more than I could deal with in my present mood.

I finished the chores and returned to the house for breakfast. I was later than usual in coming in and the table was nearly cleared and empty.

"Matilda had to eat so she could get to school on time," Mary explained without a hint in her tone that my lateness had made it difficult for anyone else.

Mary dished out two plates of pancakes and bacon and poured two cups of coffee, which she brought to the table.

"Grandpa and Uncle Charlie joined Matilda," she continued. She did not comment on the fact that she had waited for me.

I just nodded to Mary, and when she joined me at the table I said the table grace as usual.

"Anything wrong at the barn?" she questioned.

For a moment I didn't follow her, and then I realized she noticed I had taken an unusually long time with the chores.

"No," I replied hurriedly. "Just the usual. Guess I was just plain slow this mornin'. I didn't sleep too good last night for some reason."

I figured the matter was explained sufficiently and could be dropped, but Mary's eyes searched my face.

"You're not comin' down with somethin', are you?" she asked, her eyes troubled.

"Me? No, just—just somethin' I ate, I s'pose. I'm not used to eating so much before I go to bed."

Mary let it go but I could still feel her eyes on me. I didn't dare leave any of my breakfast on the plate like I wanted to.

We continued the meal in silence—there wasn't much I wanted to talk about anyway. Mary, sensing it, didn't try to involve me in meaningless conversation.

"Where's Grandpa and Uncle Charlie?" I finally asked, realizing it was strange for the two menfolk to be missing from the kitchen at that hour on a wintry day.

"Uncle Charlie went back to his room. To read, he said, but I've a notion he didn't get much sleep last night either. And Grandpa went out to the shed to work on that toboggan he's makin' for Sarah and Jon. He says the weather could turn bitter any day now, and then he won't be able to work outside."

I nodded. Yes, the weather could turn bitter. We were nearing the end of November.

After some more silence, Mary removed our plates and poured fresh coffee. She returned to her chair and sipped the hot liquid slowly. Then she put down her cup.

"Mitch stopped by while you were chorin'," she said simply and my head came around, wondering if Mitch had brought bad news. It had been some time since Mary's brother had paid us a call, and he certainly wouldn't be making neighborly calls at breakfast time.

Mary met my gaze.

"He's tired of the farm," she went on evenly, but I could see pain in her eyes. I didn't know if she was thinking of Mitch or of her ma and pa.

"He's off to the city to find himself a job. Was goin' on into town to catch the mornin' train."

I forgot my own small problems for the moment. I knew Mary needed all the sympathy and support I could give her. I could see tears glistening in her eyes, but she didn't allow them to spill over. I wished there was some way I could comfort her—give assurance that I knew it was hard for her and cared that she was hurting. But I just sat there, clumsily trying to find words, not knowing what to do or say. Finally I made a feeble attempt to reach out to her, if only by letting her talk about it.

"Did he say for how long?"

Mary's eyes lowered. "He's not plannin' to come back," she said quietly.

"I'm—I'm sorry," I muttered, reaching out to take Mary's hand resting on the checkerboard oilcloth.

"Can—can your pa manage the farm without him?" I went on.

Mary turned to me and the tears did spill over then; she clung to my offered hand as though it were a lifeline. "Oh, Josh," she said in a whispery voice, "it's Mitch I'm worried about. I've been prayin' and prayin' that he might become—become a believer. What ever will happen to him if—if he gets in with the wrong crowd in the city?"

I reached over to cover Mary's hand with my other one. "Hey," I comforted, "we can still pray. Prayer works even over long distances. There are 'right' crowds in the city too, you know. Maybe God is sending Mitch to just the right people—or person—and he will listen to what they have to say in a way that he might never listen to us."

Mary listened carefully. She was quiet for a moment and then she turned to me and tried a wobbly smile through her tears. She pulled back her hand and searched in her apron pocket for a handkerchief. After wiping her eyes and blowing her nose, she had control of herself again.

"Papa will manage—I guess," she said softly. "Mitch never did care for farm chores anyway. But Mama will be heart-broken." And another tear slipped down her cheek.

I sat there thinking of Mary—thinking of her ma and pa and their concern over Mitch.

"Did they have a row?" I asked carefully, knowing full well that it was really none of my business.

Mary smiled. "That's exactly what I asked Mitch," she answered, "but he said no, he just announced that he was leaving and they didn't even try to argue him out of it much. He said that Mama cried some—but he expected that."

Mary left the table and began preparing for washing up the dishes.

I thought about her words for a few minutes. There didn't seem to be much I could do about the whole thing.

Then an idea came to me. "Hey, why don't you go on home for a few days?"

Mary whirled to look at me, her eyes wide.

"Oh, I couldn't!" she exclaimed.

"Why not? We could manage for a few days."

"But—but the meals an' all—"

"We've made meals before." I was sure now that it was just the thing for both Mary and her mother.

"But—but Matilda—her lunch an'—"

"We'll fix Matilda's lunch. I'll do it myself—if she'll trust me."

"But I—I don't know what to say."

"Then go. Really. We can manage—as long as you don't stay away too long."

Mary was torn—I could see that. She wanted desperately to go to her mother, but she felt a deep responsibility to us.

"I mean it, Mary," I prompted further and left my chair to take the dish towel from her hands.

"Now you run off and pack yourself whatever you need

for the next few days, an' I'll go out an' hitch Chester to the sleigh."

"Are you sure?" Mary asked one last time.

"I'm sure," and I turned her gently around and urged her toward her bedroom door.

Mary left then but turned back to say over her shoulder, "But the dishes—I haven't even finished the dishes."

I looked at the dishes that remained. Mary had already washed up from the first breakfast.

"I'll do the dishes the minute I get back," I promised her, and Mary went.

As soon as she had disappeared I lifted my winter coat and hat from the peg by the door and went out to harness Chester as I had promised. Mary was out, valise in hand, just as I pulled up in front of the house. I helped her tuck in and we were off. Chester was feeling frisky, not having been used much, and he headed for the road at a fast clip. I had to slow him down to make the turn at the corner.

Mary and I didn't talk much on the way over. But we both enjoyed the brisk run in the cutter. I could sense the tension leaving Mary's body and see the shine return to her eyes. I was pleased that the idea of her spending some time at home had come to me.

As we turned down the Turley lane Mary spoke for the first time.

"How long should I stay?"

"Well—as long as you think you should," I responded slowly.

Mary smiled mischievously. "Are you trying to get rid of me, Josh?"

"Truth is," I answered, matching her mood, "I'm sorta hopin' that you'll get to missin' us real soon."

Mary's face flushed slightly, and I couldn't help but laugh.

"Seriously?" she said when her composure had returned.

"Seriously—how about until Sunday?"

"That long? This is only Wednesday."

"I know—an' I'll be counting every day—so don't be late."

Mary flushed again.

"I was wonderin'," she said after a moment, "if Matilda might like to come join me on Friday evening. She's never spent time at my house before an'—an' I think that her—her cheery mood might be good for Mama."

I pulled Chester up to the front of Mary's house. "I'll tell Matilda," I promised. "I'm sure she'd love to come and I'll bring her over."

I helped Mary out and then lifted Chester's reins again.

"Will you come in, Josh?" asked Mary.

"I think you and your mama need to meet alone," I said thoughtfully. "Besides," I went on in a lighter tone, "I've got to get on home to those dishes, remember?"

Mary laughed softly, and then grew more serious.

"Thanks, Josh," she said. "For understandin'—an'—everythin'."

I nodded and climbed back into the sleigh.

"And, Josh," Mary called softly. I turned to look at her. A few scattery snowflakes were falling about her. Some of them rested on the hair that escaped beneath her fur-trimmed hat. Her eyes were shining, her face lightened by some impulsive but pleasant thought. I waited, thinking what a picture she made as she stood there, valise in hand.

"Josh," she said again. "A motor car is nice. Really. But—but you sure can't beat a wintry sleigh ride behind Chester, can you?"

I chuckled. Mary had summed up my own feelings.

"We should do it more often," I answered. "Remind me."

And with one last grin I turned Chester around and left the lane at a fast clip. Mary was quite right. You couldn't beat a wintry sleigh ride behind Chester, and I was all set to enjoy it to the full.

But for some reason, the ride back home wasn't as pleasant as I had anticipated.

I didn't need to do the dishes when I got home. Uncle Charlie had already washed and put them in the cupboard. He had also made a fresh pot of coffee, and Grandpa had joined him at the kitchen table for a cup. When I walked in both pairs of eyes turned to me.

"Somethin' wrong, Boy?" asked Grandpa.

I poured myself some coffee and joined them at the table before explaining all about Mitch leaving and Mary's concern for her ma.

"You done right, Boy," said Grandpa. "We been hoggin' too much of Mary's time. Her ma needs her too."

Uncle Charlie just slurped his coffee and then tilted his chair on the two back legs.

"What about Matilda?" he asked at length.

"Mary wants her to come and spend the weekend," I answered. "I'm sure Matilda will be glad to."

"This is Wednesday," went on Uncle Charlie.

"We'll manage until Friday," I assured them both, and Grandpa nodded.

"I don't have anything pressing right now. Just chores. I can help in the house," I added.

Uncle Charlie hid a smile. "Never did cotton to yer cookin', Josh," he teased.

I just grinned. "Then you cook an' I'll do dishes," I challenged him.

Uncle Charlie nodded. "It's a deal," he agreed.

"We'll manage," Grandpa concluded, but I could tell by his tone of voice that he was a mite doubtful. I guess none of us realized how much we'd come to depend on Mary till she wasn't there.

Matilda was looking forward to spending the weekend with Mary and her family. The plan was for us to have our Friday supper, do up the dishes and then I'd drive Matilda over to Mary's house.

We were just finishing the cleaning up when the dog announced a visitor. It was Will Sanders again. This time he'd come by sleigh. I grinned to myself when I saw him. He certainly hadn't lost any time in making good on his promise to return, but this time he had been outfoxed. We were almost ready to leave for the Turleys'.

Grandpa opened the door and welcomed him. He came in confidently and took in the whole kitchen scene with one sweeping glance. I don't know if I just fancied it or if he really was amused to see me wiping the dishes.

"What a shame!" exclaimed Matilda. "We are just finishing up here, and then I am off to the Turleys' to join Mary for the weekend."

"I understood that Mary lives here," he responded.

"Well, she does," hastily explained Matilda, "but she's been spending a few days at home with her folks this week. She doesn't get to see much of them even though she lives so close, so Josh sent her on home for a few days."

Matilda gave the last bit of news with a hint of pride in her voice, but I think Will Sanders might well have missed the meaning of it all. At any rate, he let it go by completely and surprised me by saying to Matilda, "Then let me drive you."

Now just a minute here, I wanted to cut in, but instead I said as calmly as I could, "I already have my horse ready and waiting in the barn. All I need to do is hitch him to the sleigh."

"But mine are already hitched and waiting. No use for you to go out in the cold when I can just run Matilda on over."

He ignored my scowl and hurried right on, "I wanted to see Mary anyway."

I couldn't argue much about that.

"That's very kind," Matilda responded. "I'm sure Josh and Chester will appreciate not having to go out."

Well, I couldn't speak for Chester, but I sure knew how Josh felt about the matter. I didn't say anything, though. There didn't seem to be much point.

"Go ahead," I told Matilda. "I'll finish the dishes."

"Oh, thank you," she responded, reaching up to give me one of her impulsive little hugs right there before the eyes of Will Sanders. I was both embarrassed and smug. *So what do you think of that, Mr. Sanders?* I wanted to say, but I bit my tongue and turned back to wipe the table and rinse the dishpan.

Matilda was soon back, bag in hand and her warm coat wrapped securely around her. I didn't even watch them go, and when Matilda called, "Good night, Josh," I only mumbled in reply.

I was grumpy all evening. It was almost nine o'clock before I remembered Chester still waiting in the barn, harnessed and ready for travel. Grumbling, I lit the lantern and pulled on my heavy coat.

"Well, fella, sorry about that," I apologized as I slipped the harness from his back. "I near forgot about you. Guess—guess you an' me sorta got—stood up."

I flung the harness with extra intensity to hang it back on its pegs, and it made Chester jump.

I crossed back to him and began to gently rub his neck and his back. The ink that Jon had splashed over him had finally faded away in the sun and rain.

"Sorry, fella," I soothed. "Guess I'm just a little out of sorts. First, we've been needin' to do without Mary. It isn't easy for three fellas to batch anymore when we've been used to somethin' else. An' then this here fella comes along and takes—just takes right over with Matilda—with Mary, too."

I don't know why I expected a horse to make any sense out of what I was saying, but I went right on talking to Chester for the next five minutes. By the time I got back to the kitchen, I had settled down enough to think that I might sleep.

"Guess I'll make it an early night," I said to Grandpa and Uncle Charlie, and they didn't seem surprised. They both said good night without really looking up, and I headed on up the stairs to my room.

CHAPTER 8

Troubling Thoughts

BUT I COULDN'T SLEEP this time either. I tossed and turned and roughed up my pillow, but my mind just wouldn't let my body rest. Pixie got rather impatient with me. She left the warm spot where she always slept curled at my feet and scrambled up beside me. She whined softly, her little body wiggling slightly and her tail thumping. Then she took a lick at my face. I don't know if she was sympathizing with my misery or telling me to settle down and let her get some sleep, but I did find a bit of comfort in her seeming concern.

I reached out and ran my hand across her silky back. She let me stroke her a few times and then returned to the foot of the bed, turned a few times and lay down. I heard her yawn as she tucked in for the night. I guess she felt she had done all she could.

At last I stopped even pretending. I reached out to my night stand and felt around for the small container that held the matches, struck one and lit my lamp. Matilda had just received a stack of new dailies. I decided to get one from the kitchen and read for a while.

I was surprised when I started down the stairs to see the kitchen light still burning. I wondered if someone was ill. Then I thought of Uncle Charlie. He often got up and sat alone by the warm stove if his arthritis got too painful during the night. I decided I'd just join him for a while in the kitchen. Maybe make some hot chocolate or something.

But as I neared the bottom of the stairs, I heard voices and realized that Grandpa was up, too. I guess I hadn't been tossing for as long as I'd thought. It had just seemed like hours and hours.

"You think he's 'callin' ? " Uncle Charlie was asking.

There was a moment's silence before Grandpa responded; then I heard a chuckle. "Thet's the way I figure it, but I'll be hanged iffen I can figure out, callin' on *who*."

"Matilda?"

"Thet was in my thinkin'—at first—but he paid considerable attention to Mary the other night too. An' did ya hear him say tonight thet he wanted to see Mary?"

"Yeah—I heard 'im."

I heard a coffee cup being set on the table. A chair moved slightly on the linoleum floor. Then Uncle Charlie spoke again.

"Maybe he's jest sorta lookin' 'em both over."

"A man don't git hisself nowhere a doin' thet," observed Grandpa.

Uncle Charlie snorted. He'd been a bachelor all his life. Maybe he knew the truth of the statement. I had never thought to wonder if there had ever been a young lady or ladies in Uncle Charlie's life way back when.

"Nowhere. Thet's it exactly—nowhere," said Uncle Charlie.

" 'Course they're both awful nice girls," put in Grandpa.

"Yup. Both awful nice girls," agreed Uncle Charlie.

"Don't rightly know which one I'd pick myself."

Uncle Charlie seemed to be giving the matter considerable thought. I heard the coffee cups again.

"You know anythin' 'bout this here fella?" Uncle Charlie asked, and I could follow his line of thought. No good-for-nothin' was gonna come along and make things miserable for one of *his* girls, no siree.

Grandpa let out his breath in a raspy little sound. Finally he said slowly, "Checked a bit in town," then added quickly to try to justify himself, "Jest fer the record ya know. They say they're a fine family. Three boys. Lost both folks when the youngest was jest a tyke. Thet's Henry. Will is a couple years older. The oldest son an' his wife took in the two younger boys. Will went on to school an' then worked in the city fer a spell."

There was a moment of silence while the two men thought about Grandpa's information. Grandpa broke it.

"Couldn't find no skeletons a'tall," he admitted.

More silence. I didn't know what the emotions were down there in that kitchen—but my stomach was churnin' and my mouth went all dry. I hadn't realized it until my palms began to hurt, and then I noticed I had my fists curled so tightly that my nails were digging into them.

"Anyways—as I see it," went on Grandpa, "Josh better hurry an' make up his mind as to which girl he wants—or he's gonna be takin' the leftovers."

I felt all the air leave my lungs.

"Maybe he don't want neither," responded Uncle Charlie.

Grandpa snorted. "Iffen he don't," he said matter-of-factly, "he's dumber'n I took 'im fer."

I had long since forgotten about Matilda's newspapers. I had even forgotten about the hot chocolate. The conversation down below had my blood boilin' and was givin' me the chills—both at the same time.

"Hard choice," Grandpa was saying reflectively. "Real hard choice."

"Can't have 'em both," spoke up Uncle Charlie.

"Maybe it's been the wrong thing to have 'em both here," said Grandpa after a pause. "I mean, seein' both girls—so different—yet so—so special, an' gittin' to feel like they was more like family than—than young women to court." A long pause. "An' how in the world does a fella go about courtin' a girl thet lives in the same house as he does anyway?"

"Yeah," agreed Uncle Charlie, "an' when ya like 'em both, how do ya court the one 'thout the other feelin' left out an' such?"

"Well, this here Will don't seem to have 'im no problem—he's courtin', an' thet's fer sure."

There was silence for a minute.

"Do ya think the girls—?" began Grandpa but Uncle Charlie cut in.

"You seen an' heard 'em same as me. Any girl is flattered by courtin'."

"Do ya think they know which one he's picked?"

"I dunno. Maybe. Women have an uncanny sense 'bout thet," mused Uncle Charlie.

At the time I didn't even stop to wonder where Uncle Charlie got all his knowledge about the fairer sex.

A chair scraped against the floor. Someone was standing to his feet. I moved quickly to make my escape back to my bed, but Uncle Charlie—or was it Grandpa? no, it was Uncle Charlie, I could tell by the shuffling steps—just moved to the stove for the coffeepot.

I heard the coffee poured and Uncle Charlie sit back down. They sipped in silence for a few minutes, each busy with his own thoughts.

"Maybe Josh really doesn't care," said Grandpa.

"He cares," Uncle Charlie affirmed flatly.

"Yeah—'bout which one?"

"Can't answer thet. But he cares. It's nigh been eatin' his insides."

He sure seemed to know a lot—maybe more than I did.

"Hadn't noticed," admitted Grandpa. "How's thet?"

"Little things. He can spend the whole night tossin' on his bed. I can hear 'im. Then he gets up as touchy as a bear with cubs. I see 'im lookin' from one girl to the next—an' when thet there fella showed up tonight, Josh fairly bristled."

"Thet right? Thet right?" said Grandpa, and for some strange reason there was a bit of excitement in his voice.

I'd heard about enough. The whole thing was leaving me with a sick feeling. I moved back a step, intending to return quietly to my bed. Then a word from Grandpa caught me a blow right in the middle of my stomach.

"Jealous, huh?"

Jealous? Me? Of course I'm not jealous, I fumed. Jealousy was an evil emotion. It went right along with covetousness. My whole being rebelled against the thought.

"Iffen he's jealous—then maybe he does care. Or maybe he's jest plain-out possessive of 'em both," went on Grandpa.

"I think he cares."

" 'Bout who?"

Uncle Charlie thought for a minute. Then answered slowly, "I'm not sure thet even Josh has got thet sorted out yet."

"Well, he'd better start 'em a sortin'," Grandpa replied very seriously, " 'cause thet there young Will ain't gonna waste 'im no time."

"Yeah, he's courtin'. Fer sure he's a courtin'."

"He's a courtin' all right," agreed Grandpa again, then repeated on a still-puzzled note, "but I'll be hanged iffen I can figure out which one."

I crept back to my room, my stomach still churning and my body tight with tension. Pixie didn't even move as I eased myself back into my bed. I had been repelled by every word I'd heard. I guess that was what an eavesdropper could expect. Still, I hadn't planned to eavesdrop—it had just happened, and after the first few words I had overheard, I sure wasn't going to give myself away.

So Will is courtin'? Matilda? Or Mary? I sure hadn't been able to discern which one. *And if he's courtin', then we might lose one of the girls.* The thought was not a comforting one. Matilda and Mary seemed to sort of come as a set. And furthermore, they *both* belonged to us somehow.

But no. That was ridiculous. Even I knew that. The day would come—maybe much sooner than I liked to think—that we would lose one of the girls, or maybe both of them. We couldn't possibly keep the two of them forever. *Maybe we couldn't keep either one of them,* was a startling thought. Will would cart one of them off and then some other young buck would come along and take the other.

The very thought made my blood boil.

But *jealous*? Why would I be jealous? I mean, I had no claim to the girls—no personal claim. I'd never courted either one of them. And they certainly had not flirted with me. Well, not really. Only in a teasing sort of way.

I thought of Matilda's impulsive little embraces and my face flushed in the darkness. Then I remembered Mary reaching out to gently touch my hand, and the deep look of concern and understanding in her eyes as she did so, and I colored even deeper. *Maybe they do like me—sort of. Not just as family.* The thought was a new one and one that I had not consciously entertained before. But if—if they did—if there was any chance that they did—then I should do something about it. I mean, I didn't particularly enjoy the thought of spending my whole life as a bachelor like Uncle Charlie. I wanted a wife—love—a family.

But first—there came the courting.

I had no idea how to go about courting a girl. Oh, if it was like this here Will fella handled it, there wasn't much to it. I mean, he just came over whenever he took the notion and just sorta hung around and teased and complimented the girls some. Any fella could do that.

But, I knew that wasn't the way that I'd do it. A girl deserved more consideration than that. I thought she had a right to expect more than that. If I was courting I'd try to think of nice things to do that she might enjoy.

Take Matilda—*she loves flowers—an' sweet smellin' perfume—an' trips to town an' pretty new pieces of jewelry,* I listed off. *She likes music—and laughing and picnics in the country and drives in the motor car.* Wouldn't be too hard at all for me to think of ways to court Matilda.

What if I courted Matilda? How long did a fella have to "court" before he could properly ask a young woman to marry him? I mean, courting could take a good deal of time and expense. True, a fella could get a lot of enjoyment out of it. Especially if the young woman really enjoyed the courting—like Matilda would. Maybe she'd just want it to go on and on. *Matilda would like courtin' all right,* I decided.

But what about after the courting? I couldn't really picture Matilda in the kitchen, working over a hot stove, baking bread and canning the garden produce. I couldn't really see her leaning over the scrub board, hair in disarray while she scrubbed at dirty farm socks. Oh, Matilda fit into the courting picture just fine—but the marriage picture wasn't so easy to visualize.

Now, Mary—I could see Mary doing all those kitchen things. I had watched her perform all the household tasks dozens of times. It seemed so—so *natural* for Mary. She did it without fuss—without comment—and even seemed to somehow enjoy the doing. Mary in the kitchen seemed right reasonable. *But courtin'?* I couldn't think of a single way that one would properly court Mary. I mean, she never fussed about perfumes or pretty jewelry or lace hankies or anything like that. She never coaxed for rides in the motor car or asked for picnics. I couldn't honestly think of a thing that would make Mary impulsively throw her arms around my neck or giggle with girlish glee.

I lay there, struggling with questions I'd never faced before—working them this way and then that way. No matter how I tried I couldn't come up with any answers. But I knew instinctively that I could no longer just push the matter aside. I had to get it sorted out. My whole future depended on it.

CHAPTER 9

Eying the Field

EVEN IF I HAD wrestled with the problem for half the night, I was no nearer an answer when I got up to go choring the next morning. This much I knew, I had two girls right at hand who most young men in the area considered first-rate candidates for a marriage partner, and I had been taking them for granted.

I also knew that if I was going to choose one of them—and I figured I would be pretty dense not to—then I was going to need to decide which one and get on with the courting. The trouble was deciding. They were so different—yet both special.

Matilda's energy and enthusiasm made the house seem alive. We all enjoyed her company. Even Grandpa and Uncle Charlie counted the days until she returned from her trips home. The world just seemed like a nicer place when Matilda was around.

Then I thought of Mary. Mary was quiet—not bouncy. But Mary was—well—supportive. She was dependable and sort of comfortable to be around. I'm not sure how we would have managed without Mary.

Matilda or Mary? How was one to decide? And just what kind of tension would it put on our household if I started to court the one and left behind the other?

Now, I had no reason to think that either girl was sitting around holding her breath waiting for Josh Jones to start calling. Neither of them had led me to think they were interested in me in any other way than as a member of our household. I was maybe being presumptuous to even think that one of them would accept my small gifts and attention.

Then a new thought hit me. What if I picked a girl—Matilda or Mary—and decided to court her and she flatly turned me down? It could happen.

The thought scared me. I remembered what had happened when I had the foolish notion that I could just walk back into Camellia's life and she had announced instead that she was marrying Willie.

The idea of being rejected was so frightening that I decided, as I slopped the pigs and cared for the cows, that I would just hold back for the next several days and sorta look things over. I wanted to put out a few feelers to see if it appeared that either of the girls might favorably respond to being courted by Joshua Jones.

I was more sensitive to little things as I gathered around the breakfast table with the family that morning.

Matilda was telling a funny incident from school. One of the children had written a composition about winter. He had said in part, "The best thing about winter is that the 'moskeytoes' "—Matilda spelled it for us—"fly south to bite other people."

Matilda laughed merrily as she told it and Grandpa chuckled and Uncle Charlie grinned. Matilda was a lot of fun.

Matilda began to gather her school supplies and reach for her heavy winter wraps as soon as Grandpa had finished with our morning devotions. I had a sudden inspiration.

"Chester's in his stall," I said. "How would you like me to hitch him to the sleigh and drive you to school?"

She looked at me, her eyes big with unasked questions; then she threw her arms around my neck with a little squeal of delight.

I took that as her yes, and I grinned to myself as I shrugged into my heavy coat and headed for the barn while she finished her preparations. Maybe courting wasn't so hard after all.

It was colder and another storm was dumping more snow. I was glad I had thought of driving Matilda to school. It would have been rather miserable walking.

I tucked the heavy lap robe closely about her and we started off, Chester tossing his head and snorting, anxious to get out to the open road for a good run. Matilda leaned into the wind, anticipating the speed of the open cutter skimming over the frozen ground.

I watched her face. She loved a good run. If she had been holding the reins, she no doubt would have given Chester his head and let him run at a full gallop. As it was, I let Chester do a bit more running than I normally did, just so that I could watch Matilda's enjoyment.

When we got to the school I helped gather her things and climb from the sleigh. Her face was flushed—whether from excitement or the cold wind, I couldn't tell.

"I'll be back to pick you up after school," I promised, and she flashed a beautiful smile.

I waited long enough to see her into the school building, noting as I did so the smoke curling up from the brick chimney. The Smith boy had done his work and the potbelly stove would be spilling its welcome warmth into the room.

Matilda turned and gave me a bit of a wave just before she closed the door. I waved back and clucked to Chester, who turned smartly around and headed back out the school gate.

I felt good about the little drive to school. Oh, I hadn't made any kind of open statement or anything, but Matilda certainly had not been adverse to my company. I would just sort of keep my eyes open and see what the future days might bring.

But maybe while I was waiting, I should come up with some plan to sorta "test out" Mary.

My plan might have worked just fine had it not been for Will Sanders. I mean, the "wait and see" didn't seem too practical when he turned up on our doorstep every few days.

I still didn't care much for the guy. Grandpa's midnight discussion with Uncle Charlie kept running through my head. *He's courtin' all right,* I decided—but like Grandpa, I couldn't figure out which girl he had his eye on.

I didn't have much to say when he arrived, just sat back watching the situation. He teased and flirted with Matilda, but then he turned right around and asked Mary to a Pie Social in town. It happened to be on the night of Matilda's annual school program, so Mary turned him down. He smiled and said, "Next time" and Mary nodded her head.

When Christmas came, along with it came Will Sanders as well. He brought each of the girls a gift, a pair of warm gloves. After he finally left for home that night, the girls openly talked about it.

"I never dreamed we'd be on his Christmas list," said Matilda. "I never even thought to put his name on mine."

"Me neither," said Mary, studying the fingers of the gloves absent-mindedly. "What do we do now? I s'pose it would be terribly rude not to give a gift in return."

She looked imploringly at Matilda as though she wished her to say that it wouldn't be rude at all. Grandpa said it.

"Seems to me that one shouldn't feel obligated, things bein' as they be."

I wasn't quite sure what Grandpa meant, but I was willing to agree.

The girls kept on mulling over the problem.

"I know," said Mary suddenly. "Let's give him a gift together!"

"Together?" echoed Matilda.

"One gift—from both of us."

Matilda's face brightened. "Let's!" she squealed.

A few days later they were wrapping up a pair of socks and putting both names on the card. I won't pretend I didn't get a bit of satisfaction from the arrangement. Then it hit me—perhaps the girls didn't care too much either for the fact that Will had not openly made known whom he was courting.

On Christmas morning I unwrapped my own gifts. Matilda gave me a pair of fine cuff links. Mary gave me a hand-knit scarf and gloves set. I don't know when she ever found the time to do it without my knowing, but I sure did take pleasure in the gifts, realizing how special they were and how they bespoke the two givers.

Will Sanders, I breathed, but not aloud, *it's your turn to be jealous!*

The winter storms began to abate, and I could sense another spring just around the corner. I could hardly wait. I wanted to get back on my land. I wanted to get the Ford out again and feel the thrill of covering the miles so quickly, the wind whipping around me. As it was, I dreaded each trip to town since I had gone from the motor car back to the slow-plodding team. I put off every journey for just as long as I could.

On one such day I returned home a bit out-of-sorts because of my impatience with the snow-covered road. After caring for the team, I bundled the groceries into my arms and headed for the kitchen and a hot cup of coffee with a bit of Mary's baking.

No coffee greeted me. Grandpa and Uncle Charlie sat at the table. It appeared that they had been there for hours, not because they wanted to but because they didn't know what else to do with themselves. It was so untypical that it threw a scare into me right away.

"Where's Mary?" I asked, my eyes quickly darting about the room.

There was silence; then Grandpa cleared his throat, while Uncle Charlie shuffled his feet.

"She went on home," explained Grandpa. "Word came her ma was sick."

"Sick?" I repeated, letting the word sink in and thinking of all those years that Mary's ma had spent in bed. "How sick?"

"Don't rightly know," said Grandpa. "The youngest girl jest came a ridin' over here—nigh scared to death, and hollered fer Mary to come quick. Mary did. Without hardly lookin' back—jest jumped on up behind her an' the two of 'em took off agin."

I put the groceries down and wheeled back toward the door.

"Mary should've taken Chester," I mumbled as I went.

Grandpa called after me, "Where you off to?" Then he added as kindly as he could, "Josh, at a time like this, sometimes folks only want family."

But I didn't even slow down. "Mary's about as 'family' as you can get," I flung back over my shoulder, and Grandpa didn't argue anymore.

I didn't even wait to saddle or bridle Chester. Just untied the halter rope and led him out of his stall. In a wink I was on his back. He wanted to run and I let him. He was hard to hold in with just the halter; I guess I rode him rather recklessly. We were soon in Turleys' yard, and I flung myself off and tied Chester to the gate before hurrying to the house.

I rapped politely before entering the back porch. There was no answer so I just eased the door open and let myself in. Once in the kitchen, I took a deep breath and the doubts began to pour through me. Who did I think I was that I could intrude upon a family in such a way? Why did I dare come without invitation?

I knew instinctively that the answer to all of the questions was, "Mary." For some reason I felt she might need me. Still—I shouldn't have . . . I turned back to wait outside, but just then the younger girl, Lilli, entered the kitchen. She was wiping tears as she came, and at the sight of me she stopped short, sucking in her breath in a little gasp. Then she seemed to realize who it was and took another step forward.

"I—I'm sorry," I apologized. "I—I thought that I might—that Mary might . . . Could I go for the doc or anything?"

She shook her head slowly, the tears pouring again down her cheeks. I moved toward her but she turned her back on me, not wanting me to see her fresh outburst of tears. I hardly knew what to do or say so I just stood there, carelessly crunching my hat in my hands.

"Josh?" The little gasp that bore my name came from Mary. I wheeled to look at her, my eyes full of questions.

"Josh," she said again.

I looked into her tear-filled eyes. Her hair was disarrayed and her long skirt spattered with road grime, attesting to the fact of how she had traveled to get to the side of her ailing mother.

I moved forward. "How is she?" I asked. "Could I—"

But Mary cut me short with a tremulous voice. "She's gone, Josh."

And then I was holding her close, letting her sob against my chest. I don't know which one of us moved toward the other. Perhaps we both did.

I just held her and let her cry, and I guess I wept right along with her while my hand tried to stroke some of the tangles from her normally tidy hair. I heard my voice on occasion but all I said was, "Oh, Mary. Mary. I'm so sorry. So sorry."

At last Mary eased back from my arms. We were alone in the big farm kitchen. I looked at Mary, wondering if she was okay, wondering if I should let her go, but she just gave me a little nod and moved toward the cupboard.

"Papa needs some coffee," she said matter-of-factly, and began to put the pot on.

But Mr. Turley did not drink the coffee. I'm not sure that anyone drank from that particular pot. The whole house was too stunned—too much in pain to think of coffee or anything else.

At last I found something useful to do. I was sent to town to fetch Uncle Nat. I was both glad to go—just to get away from the intense sorrow—and sorry to go, for I hated to leave Mary in such pain.

The funeral was two days later. Mitch came home, but he stayed only a couple of days afterward and then returned to the city. Mary stayed at her home for an entire week. It seemed forever. Even when she did return to us I hardly knew what to say or do. I knew she was still sorrowing. But how did one share sorrow without probing? The only thing I could think of was to make things as easy for Mary as possible. I made sure the woodbox and water pails were kept full. I helped with dishes whenever I was in the house at the right time. I was extra careful about leaving dirty farm boots outside her kitchen—even stepped out of them before I came onto her back porch.

Whenever I saw tears forming in her eyes, I wanted to hold her again—just sort of protect her from her pain and sorrow—but it didn't seem like the thing to do. Matilda slipped her arms around her instead, and I left the room, confused and sorrowful.

Somehow we managed to get through the days until spring was finally with us again.

Chapter 10

Spring

I GAVE MY FULL attention to the land and the planting. I didn't even have time to wonder and worry about which girl I should be courting. Except on those evenings when Will Sanders showed up at our door. He still called at least once a week. I guess getting the crop in didn't cause Will as much concern as it did me.

He asked Matilda for walks and paid Mary elaborate compliments on her pies and cakes. He suggested picnics and drives. He kept promising to bring out that silver Bentley from the city. I tried to ignore him and go about my daily tasks. I was busy enough that I didn't have too much time to fret—even about Will Sanders.

Matilda began to coax about the Ford again, so on Sundays we used it to go to church and then sometimes went for a little drive in the afternoons. Matilda always wanted her share of driving. She handled the car quite well, too. Pretty soon she was asking to take it to town on her own or to take Mary home for a visit. I couldn't think of any good reason that she shouldn't, so I let her use the car. It seemed to please Matilda mightily to be behind the steering wheel.

Mr. Turley wasn't doing too well since his wife's death. In May, Faye got married as had been planned. Mary was her maid-of-honor. We were all invited to the small wedding. Mary wore a gown of soft green that brought out the reddish highlights of her hair and matched the green flecks in her eyes. I thought it most becoming on her.

Everyone tried to make the wedding a happy occasion, but we all knew that it really could not be. It was the first "big" family event that Mrs. Turley had missed, and I guess we were all thinking of her.

It was especially hard on young Lil. She knew that she would be the only girl at home now, and I think she dreaded the thought. She also was likely wondering about when it came her turn to wed—would she feel right about leaving her pa at home all alone?

I suggested to Mary that she might want to spend a few days at home after the wedding, and without argument she accepted.

She stayed for three days, and when her pa drove her back to our farm to resume her duties, he carried a large box in and set it down just inside the kitchen door.

We were all glad to see Mary back. As soon as she removed her hat she tied on her apron. The next thing she did was to stir up the fire and put on the teakettle. Mr. Turley watched her move about the kitchen. I wondered what was going through his mind. Perhaps Mary reminded him of her mother. At any rate he sure did seem to be studying her.

When the tea was ready and Mary served it up along with what was left of her orange loaf, Mr. Turley sat a long time. Grandpa and Uncle Charlie kept trying to engage him in conversation, but he answered each query scantily. He didn't seem in any hurry to leave though, and I guessed he was just stalling, hating to return to his empty house. They had dropped Lil off with a friend for a few days, Mary explained.

"Why don't you just stay on to supper?" I heard Grandpa asking.

"Got chores," mumbled Mr. Turley, and he seemed to stir himself to leave.

"Chores work up a lot faster on a satisfied stomach," argued Grandpa.

Mr. Turley nodded and settled in again.

It ended up with Uncle Charlie and Mr. Turley having a few games of checkers while Mary fixed supper. I didn't see the games, being out with my own chores, but I understand they were played rather absent-mindedly by Mr. Turley. However, they did help to pass some time.

After he had eaten, Mr. Turley still didn't seem in too big a hurry to leave. He sat toying with his coffee cup and thinking. Finally he spoke out.

"Been thinkin' on sellin' off the livestock. Mitch is gone an' there jest don't seem to be no point in spendin' time out at the barn."

I guess we all sort of looked at him, surprised at his statement. But then, we shouldn't have been.

"Anythin' over there thet you might want fer yer herd, Josh? Got one real good milker. She's had her three sets of twins already in jest five years of calvin'."

It sounded good. I nodded. "Might take a look at her," I agreed.

"Got one first-rate brood sow, too. Averages nine per litter. No runts. Though she's big, she's careful. Never laid her on a piglet yet. You know how some of 'em big sows just go 'plop' right down in the middle of the litter. Well, not this one. Coaxes 'em all off to the side 'fore she goes down."

That sounded impressive all right. I nodded again.

"Come over some time, Josh. See if there be anythin' ya'd like. Rather sell 'em to you than off fer slaughter."

I stood to my feet when Mr. Turley stood.

"You're sure you want to sell?" I asked. I still found it hard to believe.

He sighed deeply. "Yeah," he said at last. "Been thinkin' on it fer some time. Just don't cotton to the idee of spendin' hours out chorin' when the winds start to howl agin. Best time fer sellin' is when they're nice an' fat on summer grass. I'll sell 'em off gradual like an' be done with 'em by fall."

"Sure," I nodded. "Sure. I'll be over first chance I get."

"No hurry," went on Mr. Turley. "Come as soon as yer crop is all in."

Then he kissed Mary on the cheek, thanked Grandpa for supper and picked up his hat.

I felt so sorry for the man that I ached inside. I was glad I had more chores of my own that needed doing. At least they would keep me busy for a while and out of sight of Mary's sorrowful eyes.

When I came in from chores Mary had the big box up on the kitchen table and was carefully lifting something out from the wrappings to show Matilda.

"Oh," I heard Matilda gasp. "It's just beautiful!"

"I think so," Mary said softly. "Even when I was a little girl I used to admire them. They sat in Mama's buffet, and I'd look at them and look at them. Mama wouldn't let me touch them. She didn't want fingerprints all over them. Then when I got older Mama taught me how to handle them carefully. I was even given the privilege of cleaning each piece."

"How many are there?" Matilda asked.

"The large tray, a smaller tray, the coffeepot, teapot, creamer and sugar bowl, plus a sugar spoon and a cake server."

"They are beautiful!" Matilda said again.

I watched as Mary lovingly ran a hand over the silver pieces sitting before her on the table.

"Pa found a note Mama left in her Bible," she stated, tears in her eyes. "She said that I was to have the silver. She left Mitch her Bible, Lil her ruby pin, and Faye her china."

"Oh-h-h," murmured Matilda. I could tell she wanted to say how fortunate Mary was, but that hardly seemed appropriate under the circumstances.

We didn't have to wonder how special the silver was to Mary. After fondly gazing at each piece, she polished them all once more. Then she began to carefully wrap them in the soft pieces of cloth they had been snuggled in and, with tears in her eyes, placed them tenderly back in the box.

Grandpa cleared his throat. "Would ya like to put 'em there in the corner china cupboard," he ventured, "where ya can see 'em?"

Mary hesitated, looked across at the cupboard and then went to give Grandpa a little hug. I don't know what she whispered to him, but Grandpa's mustache twitched a bit and Mary began clearing a spot for her silver on the middle shelf. It did look pretty there, and it sure did dress up our farmhouse kitchen.

I guess we got rather used to it after a while, but I noticed Mary frequently glancing that way. She even used the set for tea when Aunt Lou dropped out one day, and the Sunday of Uncle Charlie's birthday she served us all our afternoon coffee from the shiny coffeepot when she served his birthday cake. Sarah thought it was just wonderful.

"Where did you get it, Aunt Mary?" she asked, her eyes shining. And Mary's eyes shone just as much as she answered.

"It was my mama's."

"I have never seen anything so pretty," went on Sarah. "Where did your mama get it?"

"It was her grandma's—a wedding present from an elderly lady she worked for. Mama said it was a shock to everyone. The older lady was usually sour and tight with her money, and no one could believe it when she gave Great-grandma such a beautiful gift."

Mary chuckled softly. It was the first I had heard her laugh for some time. She smiled often, sincerely, almost sadly, but she did not laugh. With the soft laughter a heavy weight seemed to lift from me deep down inside somewhere. I looked around the circle, wondering why there was no celebration, but no one else seemed to have noticed that Mary was laughing again.

Still I tucked the sound of that laughter away inside and replayed it over and over during the next days.

As soon as I finished the spring planting, I went over to see Mr. Turley. I ended up buying the cow he told me about plus a couple of her heifers. I also bought the sow along with the recent litter. We decided we shouldn't move her at the present, so Mr. Turley agreed to feed her for a few more weeks.

Mr. Turley carried through with his plans to sell off all his livestock, and neighbors dropped by to look over the animals and buy what they figured they could use. I thought it strange for a farmer to be without stock. But I guess the fields were enough to keep one man busy, and, as Mr. Turley had said, Mitch didn't seem inclined to come back home. It sounded as if he liked city life and was happy with the job he had found.

Lilli was restless, though. She didn't even plant much of a garden. Mary planted even more and prepared herself for a busy canning season. She went over to her ma's cellar and brought back some boxes of canning jars so she could fill them for her pa and Lil.

Matilda suggested to me that Mary might like another trip over to see Faye before her busy summer began. Mary didn't get together with her sisters nearly enough, I knew.

"I'll see what I can do," I nodded to Matilda as we sat idly swinging on the back porch swing.

It was the first we had spent any time together for several months, and with school almost out I immediately thought ahead to Matilda being gone for another summer. I wondered if I had allowed my busyness to interfere with courting again. *If I keep on at my present rate, I'll never get around to findin' myself a girl*, I concluded.

Maybe I'd lost my sense of urgency. Word passed around the neighborhood that Will Sanders had decided he preferred city living and had left his brother's house to return there. I felt a bit of smugness when I reminded myself of it.

My thoughts were interrupted by Matilda.

"You needn't do anything about it, Josh," she was saying. "I can drive Mary over to Faye's."

I was about to object when I realized that there was really no reason why Matilda couldn't. She could drive the car as well as I could. And Mary might not feel as rushed if I weren't hanging around, impatient to get back to some farm chores.

I nodded without saying anything, wondering if I was about to get another impulsive hug. Rather shamelessly I wondered if this time I should do some huggin' back. But the hug never came. Just then the back door opened and Mary stepped out with a tray of cold lemonade.

"Guess what?" squealed Matilda. "Josh says I can take the car and drive you over to see Faye before I leave for the summer."

Mary's eyes shone in the soft darkness, and I could see her appreciative smile. She didn't speak, but her eyes met mine and I read the thank you there. For a moment I wondered what it would be like to get a hug from Mary. And then I remembered the time when I had held her—not like Matilda, bouncing in and out of my arms with a quickness that took one's breath away. Mary had lingered, had leaned against me like a lost child, drawing strength and understanding from me. I had felt protective, needed. In spite of the sadness of that moment, I treasured the memory. Yet I couldn't really explain—

My thoughts were interrupted.

"When should we go?" Matilda was asking Mary.

Mary put the tray down and handed each of us a glass. "We don't have long," she reminded Matilda. "You have only another seven days to teach."

Had time really slipped by so quickly? It seemed that the year had just started, and here we were heading into another summer vacation.

"I know," moaned Matilda.

"I think we should go at a time when we don't have to worry about darkness," went on Mary. "Maybe Saturday."

"Saturday," said Matilda. "That sounds great!" Then she had the good grace to turn to me. "Will you need the Ford for anything on Saturday, Josh?"

I shook my head. I still had field work to do.

"Then we'll leave on Saturday morning," agreed Matilda.

Mary seemed to think carefully about it. "I guess we could," she said at last. "I could leave dinner all fixed for the men, and we'll be sure to be back in plenty of time for supper."

When Matilda went to school the next day, Mary sent a note for Faye, and Matilda sent the note home with one of the students who rode past Faye's new home. A reply stated that Faye would be watching for the two of them the next Saturday.

Saturday morning I moved the car from the shed, filled it with gas and checked the tires. One needed more air so I got out the pump and pumped it up until I was sure it was okay. Then I left the keys on the table for Matilda and went off to the field to do some summer-fallow work that needed doing.

I was interrupted midafternoon by a sudden rain squall. I studied the dark clouds for a few moments and headed in with the tractor.

I hope the girls aren't on their way home now, I thought, but the shower passed over. When the girls did not arrive, I dismissed the incident from my mind and started some evening chores.

By suppertime there still was no sign of an approaching car. I remembered Mary's words about being home in plenty of time to get supper, and I felt just a little aggravated that her visiting had put us hungry menfolk from her mind.

I went on to further chores and was surprised when Grandpa joined me at the pig barn. After making small talk for a few minutes, he turned to me. "The girls aren't home yet, Josh."

It wasn't news to me. I nodded rather glumly.

"It's past suppertime," went on Grandpa.

"Guess we can get our own supper," I grumbled. "We've done it before."

I wondered why Grandpa or Uncle Charlie weren't in the kitchen doing just that. Why should I need to do the chores, then—?

But Grandpa kicked at a fluff ball; then his eyes met mine. "It's not like Mary, Boy."

It finally got through my thick head. Grandpa was worried. I threw a look at the sky. It *was* getting rather late. *I* should have been worried. I just hadn't been thinking straight.

"I'll get Chester," I said, throwing my slop buckets down beside the pig pen. But I hadn't even gotten the saddle on Chester's back before I heard voices. Someone was "yahooing" my grandpa. I left Chester and went to see who had come and what news he had brought. It was one of the young Smiths, but he had already delivered his message, whirled his horse and was on his way back down the lane.

I started to holler at him to come back; then I noticed Grandpa still standing there, his hands lifted helplessly to the gatepost as though to steady himself. I hurried to him. His face was shaken.

"The girls—" he choked. "There's been an accident. The car flipped."

Chapter 11

An Awakening

I JUST STOOD THERE, staring at Grandpa, trying to get his meaningless words to make sense to me. I couldn't get them to connect somehow.

"Wh-what?" I finally heard myself stammer.

There was no response from Grandpa. He still clung to the post, weaving slightly as though fighting against a strong wind.

Uncle Charlie seemed to bring us both back to reality. He had hobbled out with his two canes to see what the commotion was about. He had heard the galloping horse—and I knew he realized it meant some kind of trouble. I could read it in his face when he demanded an explanation.

"What is it? Is it the girls?"

"They—they flipped the car." I mouthed the words but still did not really understand them. "The Smith kid—" But that was all I knew. I reached out a hand and squeezed Grandpa's arm.

"What did he say?" I insisted.

Grandpa shook his head as if to clear it. Still, it was a moment—a long moment—before he got his dry lips to form words.

"He said they—flipped the car."

"I know—I know," I heard myself agreeing impatiently, "but are they hurt?"

My own common sense told me that they would be hurt. I began to shake. "How—how badly—?" but I couldn't finish.

"I—I don't know," Grandpa said with a shudder. "The older boy went fer Doc. Thet's—thet's all he said."

I came alive then. Spinning around I ran for the barn, calling over my shoulder, "Where are they?"

Grandpa called back, "At Smiths'," and I raced to get to the barn and Chester. My insides felt as if they were in a vice. I was frantic for both girls, but I heard only one word escape from my lips. "Mary!"

Maybe it shouldn't have surprised me, I don't know. I probably should have been smart enough to know it all along, but it was painfully clear to me as I ran that if anything happened to Mary, I—I wouldn't be able to bear it.

Chester had stood stock-still. I guess he sensed I hadn't finished the job of properly putting on his saddle. If he had moved at all it most certainly would have fallen down under his feet somewhere. I jerked it off and thrust it aside now. I sure wasn't going to take the time to fuss with a cinch.

I threw myself across Chester's back even before we left the barn, ducking low to miss the crossbeam of the barn door. I didn't stop even to fasten the door behind me as I had been taught. I put my heels to Chester, and we were off down the lane.

It was the first time in my life that I let Chester run full gallop for any distance, but I didn't check him. He seemed to sense my agitation and took advantage of the situation. But even with the Smiths being fairly close neighbors and Chester running at full speed, the trip still seemed to take forever.

I wanted to cry but I was too frightened—too frozen. Even the whipping wind failed to bring tears to my eyes. All of my being seemed shriveled and deathly cold with fear. All I knew was that Mary had been hurt—maybe badly hurt—maybe even—*I need to get there—need to get to Mary!* my mind screamed at me.

When we came to the Smiths' lane, I forgot to rein Chester in and we very nearly didn't make the turn at their gate. Because of his speed, Chester swung wide when I turned him and ended up almost running into the fence rails. That near-accident sharpened my senses a bit, and I began to think rationally again.

I pulled Chester in and was able to get him under control as we entered the farmyard. I flung myself off his back and flipped a rein carelessly over a fencepost. I could see Doc's horse tied to a post down by the corral. I breathed a prayer for him and the girls as I raced toward the Smiths' back entry.

I guess I didn't knock—I don't know, but there I was in the Smiths' big kitchen. Mrs. Smith was clucking over the tragic event.

"—such a shame," she was saying. "Such nice young ladies, too. Just to think—"

"Where are they?" I cut in, completely ignoring any manners.

"Doc is with them," she replied, not seeming to take any offense at my rudeness.

"How—how—?" But I still couldn't ask the question.

Mrs. Smith just shook her head, motherly tears of concern

filling her eyes. I couldn't stand it any longer. I wanted to scream. Mrs. Smith was busy pouring a cup of coffee, and I knew without her even saying so that she expected me to sit down at her table and drink it. I turned my back on the table and the coffee cup, biting my lip to get some kind of control. I had to know! I had to know!

"Where are they?" I asked Mrs. Smith again, fighting to control my voice.

"The young schoolteacher, Miss Matilda, is in Jamie's room," she said slowly. "We thought that—"

"Where's Mary?" I cut in.

But I didn't get an answer. Right at that moment Mr. Smith entered the kitchen. He eased himself to a chair at the table and took the coffee that had been poured. Mrs. Smith just reached for another cup.

"A shame, Josh, just a shame," Mr. Smith said, shaking his head in sympathy. "Here ya only had thet there new car fer such a short time, an' I'm afraid thet it won't never be quite the same." At the look of horror on my face he hurried on. "Oh, Jamie and me pulled it outta the ditch with the team. Got it back right side up—but the frame—"

I couldn't believe it. Mr. Smith was bemoaning my motor car, and the girls were somewhere in the house in a condition I could only guess at, with the doctor trying to piece them back together.

"I don't care none about the car," I fairly exploded and then knew I wasn't being fair. "I—I'm sorry," I apologized. "It's just—just—what about the girls? You see," I went on, nearing Mr. Smith's chair as I spoke, "I don't even know what happened. How badly—?"

"I'm sure Doc will—" started Mrs. Smith, but I didn't even turn to hear the rest of her sentence.

Mr. Smith interrupted her. "Near as we can figure it," he said, "they was headin' home when thet there storm hit. The road likely got slippery. You know how it gets."

I nodded and Mr. Smith stopped for another sip of coffee.

I urged him on with another nod. *That storm was hours ago!* my brain was telling me.

"Well, they went off the road. The car flipped over. Miss Matilda wasn't able to go fer help. I suspect thet she has a broken leg—along with other things."

"Mary?" I asked numbly.

"She—she was pinned under the car—she couldn't go fer help either."

Pinned under the car. The words sent my world spinning. She was pinned under the car. She might be—she could be—

"Mary," I heard myself say again, but this time I was pleading. "Please, dear God, don't let Mary—"

"Too bad they had to lay there in the wet fer so long," Mr. Smith was saying. "Not many folks travel along thet road. Jamie an' me jest happened to—"

But I couldn't stand it anymore. I knew the rules. One was supposed to wait patiently until the doc had finished with the patient and given permission for you to go in to call at the bedside. *But this is Mary!* I had to know.

I headed for a door that would lead me to the inner part of the house. There were no sounds coming from anywhere but the kitchen, so I had nothing to guide me. "Josh," Mrs. Smith was calling from behind me, "Josh, you should—"

There was a stairway—and I took it. It led me to a hallway with doors leading off it. Four doors, in fact. I assumed them to be bedrooms and opened the first one. No one was in the room. I hurried on to the second. Doc was there. He was bending over the bed where someone lay quietly. I moved forward, part of me demanding that I turn tail and run.

It was Matilda. Her hair was wet and matted. Her face was bruised and had several tiny bandages. One leg, which lay partly exposed outside her blankets, was wrapped in whiteness. I guessed that Mr. Smith's diagnosis had been right.

I had never seen a human all bruised and broken before. She looked just awful.

At the sight of me she began to cry. "Oh, Josh. I'm so sorry," she sobbed. "The rain—the road just—"

Doc didn't scowl me out of the room. He even moved aside slightly. I knelt down beside Matilda and ran a hand over her tangled hair.

"It's all right," I said hoarsely. "It's all right. Don't cry. Just—just get better. Okay?"

I wanted to cry right along with Matilda, but I couldn't. My eyes were still dry—my throat was dry. I could hardly speak. I just kept smoothing her hair and trying to hush her.

Matilda seemed to quiet some. I stood to my feet and looked Doc straight in the eye. "How's—" I began. "How's—?"

"Mary?" he finished for me.

I nodded mutely.

"She's in the room across the hall," Doc said and turned his attention back to Matilda's arm.

I swallowed hard and turned back to the hallway. The first few steps made me feel as if I had lead boots. I could hardly lift my feet, and then I almost ran.

The door was closed and I shuddered as I turned the handle. Seeing Matilda had really shaken me. How might Mary look?

She had been—had been *pinned* under the motor car. I didn't want to go into the room—but I had to know. I had to be with her.

I opened the door as quietly as I could. A small lamp on the dresser cast a faint light on Mary's pale face. There was a large white bandage over one eye, and another covering most of an arm lying on top of the sheets, which were pulled almost to her chin. Two heavy quilts were tucked in closely about her body. *What are all those blankets hiding?* I asked myself. *She was pinned—*

My eyes went back to her face. So ashen. So still. Her eyes shut. Was she—? *Is she already gone?* And then I saw just the slightest movement—almost a shiver.

In a few strides I was beside her, kneeling beside her bed, my hand reaching to gently touch her bruised face.

"Oh, Mary, Mary," I whispered.

Her lashes lifted. She focused her eyes on my face. "Josh?" she asked softly.

"I was so scared," I admitted as I framed her cheek with my hand. "I was afraid I'd lost you—that—"

"I'm fine," she whispered, moving her bandaged arm so that she could reach out to me.

"Don't move," I quickly cautioned, fearing she might come to more harm.

"I'm fine," she assured me again in a whisper.

"But—but you were pinned—"

"Miraculously pinned," Mary responded and she even managed a weak smile. "Oh, it caught me a bit on the arm—but it was mostly my coat sleeve. Doc says I'm a mighty lucky girl."

"You're—you're not hurt?"

Mary moved slightly, and groaned. "I didn't say I'm not

hurt," she admitted; then seeing the look of panic in my eyes, she quickly went on, "But nothing major and nothing that won't heal."

"Thank you, God," I said, shutting my eyes tightly for a moment. Then I turned my full attention back to Mary. "I was so scared—so scared that—that—I didn't even know until—until Billie brought the word—"

"I'm sorry, Josh. We had no way of getting help. No way of letting you know. We couldn't get to a neighbor's. Couldn't even get to the road an'—your supper—?"

I stopped her. The memory of my impatience over our meal not being ready made me flush with shame. I looked at Mary's face, swept soft and pale in the lamplight. "I should have known. I should have realized before," I admitted. "I don't know how I could be so dumb."

"You had no way of knowin'," argued Mary. "Sometimes we are later than we plan. Things—things just happen that delay us. But to miss the supper hour—No one could have guessed that we were lyin' there in the ditch," Mary explained and I realized that once again she was finding excuses for me. She was always doing that. Getting me off the hook when I did or said something stupid.

I brushed a wisp of hair back from her face. "Maybe deep down inside I knew all the time," I murmured, "but it took something like this for me to realize—"

Mary's eyes were puzzled. "You couldn't have known 'bout the accident," she said.

"No," I answered. "I'm talkin' 'bout me—us. I was scared to death, Mary, that I'd lost you—before I'd really found you. I didn't realized until—until—" I stopped with a shudder.

"Josh," said Mary softly but insistently, "what are you talkin' about?"

I looked at her—my Mary, lying there white and quiet on the neighbor's borrowed bed. *She could have been killed!* My heart nearly stopped even at the thought. *I could have lost her. But she is still here.*

I tried to speak but I choked on the words. I swallowed hard and tried again, looking directly into Mary's eyes.

"I—I love you," I managed to blurt out. "Maybe I always have—at least for a long time, but—but I was just too blind to see it—until now. I—"

But Mary's little whisper stopped me. "Oh, Josh," she uttered, her hand coming up to touch my cheek, and I could see tears filling her eyes.

My own tears came then. Sobbing tears. I laid my head against Mary's shoulder and wept away all the pent-up emotions of the past dreadful hours. Mary let me cry, her hand gently stroking my head, my shoulder, and my arm.

I didn't bother to apologize when I was finished. Somehow I knew Mary wouldn't think an apology necessary.

"I love you," I repeated, conviction in my voice.

"Bless that ol' car," Mary said with a little smile.

"What?"

"Bless that car. An' the rain. An' the slippery road. An' our upendin'." Mary was smiling broadly now, but her words made no sense at all. I wondered if she maybe was hallucinating.

"Oh, Josh!" she exclaimed, her eyes shining, "you don't know how long I've wanted to hear you say those words."

"You mean—"

"I have loved you—just *forever,*" she stated emphatically. "I began to think that you'd never feel the same 'bout me."

I felt as if there was a giant explosion somewhere in my brain—or in my heart. *I love Mary. Mary loves me back!* She would get better. We could share a life together. I could ask Mary to be my wife.

I had to put it in words—at least some of it. "You love me?"

Mary nodded. "Always," she stated simply.

"And I love you—so much."

Mary nodded again, her face flushed with color.

"Then—" I began, but stopped. I hesitated. It didn't seem fair to her somehow. Slowly I shook my head.

"No, no," I said. "I'm not gonna ask you now. Not yet. I'm gonna court you properly. Give you a little time."

A small question flickered in Mary's eyes.

"But not much time," I hurried on. "I couldn't stand to wait long now—now that I know. And one thing you can be sure of—I'm gonna come askin'—so you'd best be ready with an answer."

"Oh, Josh," Mary whispered.

Doc's timing couldn't have been worse. I had just kissed Mary—for the first time—and found it quite to my liking. Knowing now that she wasn't seriously injured, I drew her a little closer. Mary's eyelashes were already fluttering to her cheeks in anticipation of another kiss, her arms tightening about my neck. I don't know if it was the opening of the door or Doc's "ahem" that brought me sharply back to reality, but I sure did wish he could have delayed just a few minutes more.

CHAPTER 12

Courtship

WHEN I GOT BACK down to the kitchen, Grandpa and Uncle Charlie had arrived as well as Uncle Nat. Everyone was concerned about the girls, and the talk in the room was hushed and stilted.

But I wanted to shout and skip around the room like Pixie used to do. It seemed impossible that just a half hour earlier I'd had the scare of my life. Now I was walking on air. With all my heart I wished that I could share my good news—but I knew that wouldn't be right. Especially when Mary couldn't be with me. Yet I was fairly giddy with my new-found love. I felt several sets of eyes on me, and I wondered if they could see right through to my heart. I fought hard for some composure.

"They're fine," I said as nonchalantly as I could. "Both of 'em. Only scratches and cuts and bruises and a broken leg."

I knew that description didn't exactly go with "fine"—but

I guess the group around the kitchen table was willing to chalk it up to my relief.

"Thank God!" said Grandpa, and Uncle Nat echoed his words. Then we were all bowing our heads while Uncle Nat led us in a prayer of thanksgiving. As soon as we had finished our prayer they wanted a more complete report.

"So Miss Matilda's leg *was* broken," Mr. Smith pointed out with a knowing glance around the room.

I nodded.

"What else?" prompted Grandpa, referring to Matilda again. "What other injuries? Is she hurt bad?"

"Just cuts and bruises. Nothin' that won't quickly heal. She was worryin' about the motor car." I was still uncomfortable that she would even think about that when all I wanted was for the two girls to be alive and well.

"An' Mary?" asked Uncle Charlie, his voice quivering a bit.

At the mention of Mary's name, my heart leaped in my chest and I was sure my face must be flushing.

"She's fine—just fine." I couldn't keep some excitement from creeping into my voice no matter how hard I tried. "She—she has some cuts—one above her eye, one on her arm. Lots of bangs and bruises—but not even a broken bone." They were all so intent in their worrying over the girls that they missed my intensity. Anyway, no one looked at me like I expected them to look. They just muttered words of relief and joy and glanced at one another with a great deal of thankfulness.

"She was pinned," insisted Mr. Smith, who must have told them that Mary, having been pinned under the automobile, could be in serious condition.

"Doc says she was lucky," I explained. "It was mostly the

sleeve of her coat that was pinned to the ground. Oh, her arm is cut some—but it could have been bad—really bad."

There were murmurs again.

"Now, Josh, you just sit yerself right down here and drink a cup of coffee," Mrs. Smith was saying. "You are 'most as pale as a ghost."

All eyes turned back to me. And then the funniest thing happened. The whole world began reeling and spinning like you'd never believe. I felt myself a-reeling and spinning right along with it. But I didn't seem to be keeping up somehow—or else I was going faster. I tried to walk to the chair that Mrs. Smith had indicated, but my feet wouldn't work. Besides, the chair had moved. I didn't know what was happening to me.

I guess Uncle Nat caught me. I really don't remember. I came to my senses on Mrs. Smith's couch with Doc bending over me and a whole cluster of people hovering near. It took me awhile to realize what was going on, and then I felt like a real ninny. I mean, it was the girls who had been hurt in the accident and here I was doing the passing out.

I struggled to sit up, but Doc reached out a restraining hand.

"Take it easy, Josh," he cautioned. "You've been through quite a bit tonight."

Was it my imagination or was there a bit of a chuckle in Doc's voice? I remembered the scene that he had walked in on upstairs, and I felt my face flush. But no one else seemed to notice.

"Mrs. Smith is bringing some broth and crackers," Doc said. "You probably didn't have any supper."

I refused to be fed like a child, though I did obey Doc and sat up slowly. Then I carefully spooned the broth with its crumbled crackers to my mouth. My head soon began to clear and things came into focus again. With the return to awareness came the recollection of my recent discovery, and I could scarcely conceal my excitement.

As soon as I was able to convince Doc that I could walk a straight line, I stood to my feet.

"Can I see Mary—the girls—again?" I asked.

"Matilda is already sleeping—and Mary might be, too. I gave her a little medicine to help. You can peek in on her—but just for a moment. You hear?"

There was a twinkle in Doc's eyes and I caught a quick wink. I flushed and nodded, then headed for the stairs.

Mary was almost asleep when I crept quietly to her bedside.

"Doc says I can say good night," I whispered, "but I'm not to stay long."

Mary gave me a dreamy smile—brought on more by the sleeping powder than by my presence, I was sure.

"How are you feelin'?" I asked, taking her hand.

"Sleepy," she murmured.

I kissed her fingers.

"You're not backin' out on me, are you?" I teased. "Haven't changed your mind, now that you've had a little time to think on it?"

Mary tried a smile. It was weak and lopsided in her relaxed state. Fighting hard to keep her eyes open, she squeezed my hand. "You don't get off that easy, Josh," she teased back. "I'm holdin' you to your word."

I leaned over and kissed her. "I love you, Mary," I told her again. "That's never going to change."

She stirred and tried to smile again. Sleep had almost claimed her.

I knelt down by her bed, my arm around her blanketed form, my other hand still holding hers.

"Go to sleep," I whispered. "I'll stay with you until you do."

She moved her head so her cheek rested against mine and then she sighed contentedly. It was only moments until her even breathing told me she was sleeping soundly. I leaned to kiss her forehead before standing to my feet.

She slept so peacefully, so beautifully. *Even with bandages and bruises, she's the most—the most lovely girl in the world, my Mary,* I thought. I could hardly wait for the time when she would be well and whole again—for the real courting to begin.

"Good night, Mary," I whispered. And then after a quick look around to see if Doc was lurking in the doorway, I tried a new word I'd never used before, just to see how it sounded. "Good night, sweetheart."

It sounded just fine.

Matilda's folks hired a motor car to come and take her home where her mother could nurse her back to health again. Since school was nearly out for the summer anyway, they just let the kids go a little earlier than usual.

Mary went back home to her pa and sister Lilli. I missed her something awful at our house, but it did make things a bit easier for me in regards to courting. Like I said before, how does one go calling on someone who is right there in your own house? Mary said that her being home with her pa right now was working out good because it would help to keep tongues from wagging. I hadn't even thought on that, but if it made Mary feel more comfortable with the courting, then I was quite happy to put up with batching it for the summer months.

I was in for a great deal of good-natured teasing when family and friends learned that I was actually courting Mary. I didn't mind. In fact, I rather enjoyed it. I didn't see Mary objecting much to it either. It was rather nice to be known as a couple. Made us feel that we really belonged to each other in some way.

I took a hammer and mallet to the frame of the Ford and to the fender dents. It wasn't a good job, but when I was done she could at least stand on four wheels and make it slowly down the road again. I even bought some paint and touched up the scars, but she never did shine and sparkle the same. I will admit that I sure didn't like the way she looked, but to my surprise it really didn't matter as much as I had thought it would. *And,* I reminded myself, *the accident, dreadful as it was, had brought Mary an' me together.*

In the absence of Mary, Uncle Charlie took over the kitchen duties again. His cooking wasn't near as good as it used to be. I suppose there were times I might've even been tempted to complain a bit—but I wasn't noticing much what I was putting in my stomach anyway. I was far too busy thinking of Mary.

Every day that I was able to finish up my work early enough, I chugged over in my beat-up Ford to call on her. I brought her field flowers that I knew she admired. I kept finding little things in town to bring a shine to her eyes. I picked the produce from her garden and toted it over so that she and Lilli could can it for fall. I tucked a member of the new litter of kittens in my shirt as soon as its mama had weaned it and took it over to Mary as a surprise. I brought news of Grandpa and Uncle Charlie and shared bits of information about the farm and clippings on garden care from the farm paper. And we spent hours just talking—about our plans, our dreams, our goals, and getting to know each other better.

I was hoping for a fall wedding. Just as soon as the harvest was in and the fall work was done. But I hadn't yet mentioned that to Mary. I was waiting for just the right time. It seemed to me that the right time would be somewhere in the first part of August—after the haying was done and before I went full tilt into harvest. That would give me time to shop carefully for a ring—maybe even go into Crayton. It would also give Mary time to make her wedding plans after she had said yes.

But before all that could take place, I had to ask her pa for Mary's hand in marriage. I wasn't worried about the prospect. I was confident that Mr. Turley would not hesitate in giving us his blessing. He had already indicated as much on more than one occasion. Still, I planned to fit in with all of the social obligations and do my courting in the proper fashion.

I fervently hoped and prayed that all the farm work would move along properly so that as much of my time as possible could be spent with Mary and so that none of the fall work would delay our plans. Things did go along quite well until we hit mid-July. I had been sweating over the haying, hurrying it up so that I might pass on to the next stage of the work. Just getting from one task to the next seemed to somehow hurry the days along until I could be with Mary.

But rain stopped the scheduled progress. Gazing at the foreboding sky, I sensed it was going to be more than just a shower. I felt awfully agitated as I steered the tractor through the gate and headed for its shed. I cast another look at the sky. From one horizon to the other, dark, ominous clouds hung above me with no break in sight.

I thumped a fist against the steering wheel. *The dumb weather is going to go and throw everything off schedule!* I fumed.

I did the chores in a sullen mood and went in for supper.

Uncle Charlie was serving up his tasteless stew—again. I couldn't help but think of Mary's cooking. The roasts, the biscuits, the gravy. Then my eyes noticed big pieces of peach pie sitting on the counter.

"Where'd the pie come from?" I asked, knowing without asking that it wasn't Uncle Charlie's doing.

"Mary brought it over. She came to pick the beets."

Mary had been here—and hadn't even waited to see me.

"She was goin' to take ya some lunch in the field, but thet dark cloud came up an' she knew she had ta beat it home," explained Grandpa.

I nodded then, simmering down some.

I ate the stew, all the time thinking ahead to that pie.. It was just as good as I knew it would be. My longing for Mary increased with each mouthful, not because of the pie itself. It was just a reminder of how much I missed her.

After supper I sorta kicked around. I helped with the dishes, noticing how careless we were about keeping the big, black stove shined up. I made a hopeless botch of sewing a patch on my faded overalls. I tried reading the farm magazine, but the words wouldn't sink into my thick skull. Finally I gave up. Scooping up Pixie, I headed upstairs for bed. But I couldn't sleep. I just kept thinking about Mary. Pixie seemed to know that something was bothering me. She licked at my hand and whimpered softly.

"Sorry, Old Timer," I said, swallowing my frustration. "I just miss her. So much. I know that courtin' is s'posed to be a special time—yet I keep thinkin' that if it wasn't for courtin', she could be here now where she belongs—with us. I don't know how much longer I can stand this—this waiting."

It wasn't that Pixie was unsympathetic—but she was getting old. I guess she figured that she deserved a good sleep even if

I couldn't manage one. She took one lick at my cheek and then excused herself, settling in at her customary spot at the foot of the bed.

I lay there in the darkness, hurt and lonely, angry with the rain that still relentlessly pounded the roof above my head. *It's slowin' down everything,* I reasoned unrationally. *I'll have to wait even longer for Mary.*

The next day it continued to rain. I wanted to go to see Mary, but I decided my mood was so sour that I'd better keep to myself.

In the evening I moped around again. I don't know how Grandpa and Uncle Charlie put up with me. Finally I motioned to Pixie and headed for bed.

She didn't spend much time sympathizing that night. She must have figured it was my problem. After one lick on the cheek she found her way slowly to the foot of the bed and settled herself in with a deep sigh.

I lay there listening to the wind and the rain and hating both of them along with my own feelings. I couldn't sleep. I tossed and turned and sweated and shivered by turn. Grandpa and Uncle Charlie finally went to bed. I saw the light pass by my door, and then I was in total darkness. At last I could stand it no longer. I crawled from bed and pulled my pants back on. I shrugged into my shirt and grabbed my socks and shoes. I knew I would be quieter going down the stairs barefoot.

I heard Pixie stir and whine a bit as though she was asking what in the world I was up to, but I didn't even stop to stroke her soft head. I couldn't stand it one minute longer. I was going to see Mary.

Chapter 13

Plans

I DIDN'T EVEN HAVE the good sense to put on my slicker. Before I reached the barn I was soaked. The water ran down the brim of my hat and dripped down the back of my neck. The wind lashed against my body, sticking my pant legs to my limbs and whipping my chore coat tightly against me.

I didn't dare try to drive the car in this weather. Chester had been given the freedom of the pasture and rarely ever fed near the barn. But one of the work horses was humped up against the corral fence, back to the storm and head hanging down. I called to him and moved to open the barn door. The horse was only too glad to hurry in out of the wind and rain.

I felt almost like a traitor when, instead of producing a scoop of grain, I slipped a bridle over his unsuspecting head. He didn't fight it but he must have been disappointed.

I had to walk him every step of the way. As I had guessed, the road was already slippery and he wasn't nearly as sure of foot as Chester. Besides, the heavy clouds made the night so black one could scarcely see the trees by the side of the road.

"Why didn't I just walk?" I mumbled to myself as we trudged along, but even with my question I knew that the horse was better at picking his way through the mud than I would have been.

There was no light in the Turleys' windows when I turned old Barney down the lane. I knew they would have all retired long ago, and half my mind kept urging me to turn the horse around and go home in sensible fashion. But I couldn't. I just couldn't. The other part of me said I had to see Mary.

I slipped the reins over Barney's head and flipped them around a fence post. Even to get across the yard was a chore. I slipped and slid my way to the house. My teeth were chattering and my whole body drenched. I'd probably catch my death of cold—but now wasn't the time to be worrying about that.

Rather than pounding on the door and waking the whole household, I went directly to Mary's window. I tapped with my fingers on the glass, wondering if she would hear as she slept.

But the blind responded almost immediately and the curtain was lifted back from the pane.

"Who is it?" Mary called softly.

As should have been the case long before now, I felt like a complete fool. *What in the world am I doing? What on earth will Mary think?* My thoughts and emotions tumbled together. *And her pa?* If he had been willing to give his consent, he surely would change his mind now. I wanted to bolt and run for cover, but I didn't. I just couldn't. I had to see Mary.

"It's me. Josh," I said as clearly and quietly as I could, so Mary would hear me but her pa wouldn't.

"What is it? What's wrong?" Mary's voice faltered, and I

realized for the first time that of course she would come to that conclusion.

"No. No, nothing," I quickly assured her. "I—I just had to see you—that's all."

Mary hesitated for just a moment. "Go to the door," she told me. "I'll be right there."

And she was, with a heavy housecoat wrapped firmly about her. She held the door for me and then gasped.

"Oh, Josh. You are soaked to the bone. You'll catch your death!"

I couldn't deny it, so I just shrugged.

"Get out of those shoes and socks," she ordered, just the right amount of authority in her voice. "An' that coat!" she added. "I'll be right back."

I laid aside my dripping hat and pulled myself free of the rain-heavy coat. I pulled off the soggy shoes and tugged away the sodden socks. Embarrassed, I noticed the terrible mess that I was making of the Turley entry.

Mary was back just as the last sock came off. In her arms were some dry clothes and a rough towel.

"Mitch left them," she explained. "Use his bedroom and get out of the rest of those wet things. I'll put on some coffee."

"But—but I'll leave a trail all across your floor," I said hesitantly.

"A trail I can wipe up. Now hurry," urged Mary.

I hurried. Actually it was rather fun to be bossed by Mary.

It didn't take me long to towel myself dry and slip into the borrowed clothes. But I was still shivering as I headed back to the kitchen.

"Your pa's gonna want my hide," I said through chattering teeth as I held my hands up to the newly fanned fire.

"My pa would sleep through a hurricane," answered Mary as she placed the coffeepot on the stove.

"He would?"

"He would."

Mary had returned to her room while I had been changing and was now fully dressed. She'd even taken the time to tie her apron carefully over her kitchen frock. I noticed, though of course I didn't comment, that Mary was not wearing one of her Sunday frocks as she normally did when I came calling and that her hair was not as neatly groomed as usual. She had simply tied it back from her face with a ribbon.

"If nothing is wrong—with anyone," she said carefully, not looking at me from her place at the stove, "do you mind telling me what brings you out on such a night as this?"

I held my breath. Was there just a trace of scolding in Mary's voice? Was she angry with me? She had good reason to be. I waited a moment. Mary waited also.

"I—I couldn't sleep," I answered lamely.

Mary swung around to get a look at me. She must have thought I'd taken leave of my senses. The scar across her forehead from the accident showed faintly in the lamplight. It reminded me of how close I had come to losing her.

"You—you couldn't *sleep*?" she echoed and turned back to put another stick in the fire and needlessly shift the coffeepot.

There was more silence. Mary broke it. "That seems—seems like a rather—rather poor reason to be out ridin' in a drenching rain, Josh," she said quietly.

"It—it is," I admitted. Then I hesitantly went on, "Except that I knew the reason I couldn't sleep was because—because I needed to see you."

Mary stirred slightly but she didn't turn around to face me.

"I—I missed you," I stammered to a conclusion.

I saw Mary's back stiffen slightly. "You could have told me that at a sensible hour, Josh," she reminded me.

She *was* angry with me. Mary, who never got angry with anyone—who always found some reasonable explanation for the dumb things I did—who fought for me, defended me. She was angry—and I had never had Mary angry at me before.

Rooted to the spot, I was unable to decide what to do next. I should never have come—not at such an unearthly hour, not in the rain that dripped muddy puddles all over her floors. I had been inconsiderate and stupid. I had been thinking only of my loneliness—not the feelings and rights of Mary.

But Mary was speaking again—and there was a tremor in her voice. "I waited for you all last evening—all this evening. I knew you weren't busy. There was nothin' you could do in the rain. But you didn't come. An' finally I—"

But I had stopped listening to the actual words and was hearing the meaning loud and clear. Mary wasn't angry with me because I had come. She was angry with me because I hadn't come *sooner*.

I looked at her straight, slim back with the neatly tied apron, the gently sloped shoulders set in a plucky line, the head stubbornly lifted. It was enough to propel me forward silently, swiftly. I slipped my arms around her and buried my face in her hair. Tears came to my eyes, though I don't really know why.

"Mary," I whispered, "I came because I couldn't stand being without you any longer. I was so upset about the weather I didn't want to come and burden you with it all. But I—I can't bear it without you. I—I want you to marry me—as soon as possible.

I can't stand being apart like this. Please, please forgive me for coming so late but—"

Mary turned in my arms. She was looking directly at me when I opened my eyes.

"Oh, Josh!" she cried. "Yes. Yes," and her tears mingled with mine as she pressed her cheek against my face.

I don't know how long I might have gone on holding her, kissing her, had not the coffeepot boiled over. With a little cry Mary jerked away from me and rescued the pot.

"Sit down," she said, wiping her eyes with a corner of her apron and nodding toward a kitchen chair. She hurried to clean up the stove and pour the coffee.

She pulled her chair up next to mine and rested her chin in her hand. "Now, sir, you were saying—?" she teased.

I laughed right along with her. Then I sobered. "I—I guess I was asking you to marry me and not in the most orthodox way," I admitted. "Not at all like I had planned. I've just gone and ruined the whole thing. I—I mean—I had these great ideas. I spent hours thinking about it. Selecting just the right words. Not just—just blurting it out." I stopped and shook my head. "I'm—I'm sorry," I whispered.

Mary reached out a hand and touched my cheek. "Sorry? Sorry for missing me? For loving me?"

"For spoiling what should be one of your most treasured memories. For blundering into something that should be very special."

"Josh," said Mary softly, her eyes filling with tears and her voice soft with emotion, "I have just been told that I am loved. I have been asked if I will share your life—for always. Josh, it doesn't get any more special than that."

A tear slid unchecked down Mary's cheek. I reached out a finger and brushed it away.

"I don't even have the ring," I confessed.

"You'll get it soon enough," Mary defended me.

"I—I haven't even spoken to your pa."

"He'll give his blessing."

Then I took a deep breath. "That's not all," I admitted slowly as Mary waited. "I—I don't want to wait," I burst out. "Not till after harvest. Not a month. Not even a week if—"

Mary's eyes flew wide open.

"I know it's not fair. That it's terribly selfish. But you won't come home until we are married and I guess I couldn't bear it even if you did—but honestly, Mary, I don't want to wait any longer to get married. I know—I know it's not reasonable, that a girl needs lots of time to make her dress and sew her pillowcases and—and do whatever else it is that girls do, but—"

"Sunday?" said Mary.

"We really don't need a big fancy cake an' all the trimmings, and we've got pillowcases, an' you could wear that pretty blue—"

"Sunday?" said Mary again.

I frowned, not understanding.

"I think I could be ready by Sunday if you can," Mary said calmly.

"Sunday? Which Sunday?"

"Next Sunday."

"*Next* Sunday?"

"This is Tuesday," said Mary, laughter in her voice. "That leaves us Wednesday, Thursday, Friday and Saturday. Then comes Sunday. I can be ready by Sunday."

"By Sunday? Next Sunday?" I stammered.

"Are you trying to back out?" she teased.

"Of course not. I—I just supposed that you'd need—"

"You told me already that you planned to propose—remember? Well, there is no cake or dress ready—*yet*. But Lou said she would bake the cake, and I did find a piece of lovely material and I'm really quick with a sewing machine. Both Faye and Lilli will help. They promised. And as for the pillowcases, Josh—that is the *one* thing that *is* ready."

Neither of us had paid any attention to the cups of coffee that now sat cool and unwanted before us. I pushed my cup farther away so I wouldn't tip it over when I put my arms around Mary.

"Sunday," I grinned. "Sure. Sunday." Then my mind began to whirl. I had a few things that needed doing before Sunday, as well. How in the world would I get it all done in time? First thing in the morning I'd need to head out for that ring. Two rings, in fact. Then I'd—I'd—well, I'd talk to Uncle Nat and Aunt Lou, that's what I'd do. They'd have a whole list of things I needed to attend to. I had no idea.

Mary stirred. "Pa?" she said.

"You said he'd sleep through a hurricane," I reminded her.

"And so he would," Mary smiled, ruffling my still-wet hair, "but not through the marriage of one of his daughters. You'd best try to get a comb through that hair while I go wake him," and she kissed me on the nose and went off.

My head started working again. "Barney," I muttered. "I didn't care for Barney." I looked about the kitchen for a slicker, not wishing to get a soaking again. Mitch might not have left anything else behind.

I spotted a slicker belonging to Mr. Turley and took the

liberty of borrowing it just long enough to lead the horse in out of the rain and toss a bit of hay in the manger.

When I returned to the kitchen I managed to comb my hair and smooth some of the wrinkles out of Mitch's worn shirt. There was nothing I could do about the short legs on my pants. Mitch wasn't quite as tall as I was.

Mary and Mr. Turley arrived in the kitchen together a few minutes later. He still looked sleepy and confused, but Mary was radiant. She had changed her dress to the pretty blue one I had referred to earlier. Her hair was carefully pinned up, too. She gave me an encouraging smile, and I took a deep breath and began my little speech.

"Sir, I realize that this is an untimely hour, and I apologize for that—but I would—would like to ask for your daughter Mary's hand in marriage, sir. I—I love Mary deeply and she has—has honored me by returning the love, sir, and—"

I guess Mr. Turley had heard enough or maybe he was just anxious to get back to bed. He reached out and shook my hand vigorously. "I'd be proud, Son," he said huskily. "I'd be proud." Then in a slightly choked voice, he added, "It woulda made her mama very happy."

Mary slipped an arm about me and gave me a squeeze and then she ran off to waken Lilli and tell her the good news.

No one went back to bed that night, not even Mr. Turley. We stayed up until the sky began to lighten. The sun never did come out because of the clouds, but I didn't mind them anymore. We talked the night away, making our plans for the coming wedding. Then with the daybreak I kissed Mary good-bye, borrowed Mr. Turley's slicker again and mounted Barney for the trip back home.

I got home before Grandpa or Uncle Charlie had left their

beds. Pixie was waiting for me, though, sniffing at the door, a confused look in her eyes.

I picked her up and held her close. "Pixie," I told her, "I'm getting married. Not 'sometime,' but Sunday. *This* Sunday." Then I threw all caution to the wind and bellowed for the whole house to hear. "I'm getting married! Sunday! This *next* Sunday. You hear! *I'm getting married!*"

CHAPTER 14

Sunday's Comin'!

I SURE WAS RELIEVED when it stopped raining. I had lots of plans to make and traveling to do, and it would have been most miserable trying to do it all in the pouring rain.

As it was, the roads were rutted and muddy, so it was out of the question to use the motor car. Mostly I rode Chester, and the horse heard many declarations of love that week. Even if they weren't meant for him.

I don't know what I would ever have done without help from Uncle Nat and Aunt Lou. Even Grandpa and Uncle Charlie lent a hand—mostly doing up my chores while I ran about. They were 'most as excited as I was.

I asked Avery to be my best man. A lump came into my throat as I made my choice. I knew Willie would have been standing at my side had things turned out differently.

Mitch would have been my second choice—mostly for Mary's sake, but Mitch sent back word that he wouldn't be able to make it by Sunday, and he gave Mary and me his best wishes. So I went to call on Avery and he grinned from ear to ear as he accepted my invitation.

Mary picked Lilli to be her maid of honor, and she was pretty excited about it too.

True to her word, Aunt Lou made the cake. She also organized some of the church ladies who offered to serve a meal following the ceremony. Everyone seemed anxious to help out, and I knew that some of the reason was because Mary had lost her mama.

Even Sarah got involved. "Mama says I can serve the punch, Uncle Josh," she informed me and I gave her a hug and told her I knew she'd do a great job.

On Thursday I made the long trip to get the rings since our little town did not have what I considered suitable for Mary. How I wished for better roads and the automobile, but Chester did the best he could. We were both tired when we got home that night; even so I cleaned up and headed for Mary's house. I figured Chester had used his legs enough for one day, so I walked. It wasn't that far to Mary's if you cut across the pasture.

She looked a bit surprised when she opened the door to my knock.

"Expectin' someone else?" I bantered.

"No, Josh," she laughed, drawing me in. "But I wasn't expectin' you either. I thought you'd be far too busy to come callin'."

"I was," I teased. "I am—but I thought you might like to have this before Sunday." I held out the little box that held her ring.

Mary gave a little gasp and reached out her hand. I pulled the box back. "Not so fast," I told her. "You haven't yet told me what a wonderful guy you'll be marryin' come Sunday."

Mary glanced back at the table behind her. I could see bits and pieces of soft white material scattered over it.

"If you don't stop pesterin' me and be on your way, there won't be a wedding," she warned me. "No dress—no wedding."

I turned to look more closely at the table, but Mary put a hand over my eyes.

"No peeking," she commanded. "It's not fair to see the dress before the ceremony."

"Then come out to the veranda," I suggested.

"For only a short time," Mary insisted, pretending she wasn't interested in the little box, as she allowed herself to be led to the veranda bench.

I seated Mary, then dropped to one knee in front of her. I reached for her hand and spoke softly, "Mary Turley, would you do me the honor of becoming my wife—Sunday next?" I added with a hint of a smile.

Mary reached out to ruffle my hair, then changed her mind and let her hand fall to my cheek. "That would make me the happiest girl in the world," she said, her gentle smile saying even more than her words.

I caught her hand and kissed the palm—then opened the small box and removed the ring. Carefully I slipped it on Mary's slender finger. "Oh, Josh," she murmured, lifting the ring to study it and then brushing it against her lips, "it's beautiful."

She leaned forward to kiss me as I knelt before her.

"Now go finish that dress," I prompted. "I don't want any excuses come Sunday."

But we lingered for a while, just talking about our plans and comparing progress. It was dark before I headed back across the fields for home. I whistled as I walked in the light from the moon. I had never been happier. I had just placed my ring on Mary's finger, and Sunday promised to be the greatest day of my life.

We were to be married immediately following the Sunday morning service. Everything, as far as I knew, was in readiness. I would wear my wedding suit to church. Mary and Lilli would slip out and change at Lou's just as soon as the service ended. Lou had things well in hand for our reception dinner with the help of the parishioners. Mary's silver service had been polished to perfection and stood ready and waiting to serve the guests. I knew the silver pieces were far more than a teapot and coffeepot to Mary. They were a small symbol of her mother at our special occasion. I also knew that Mary would miss her mama even more intensely on her wedding day.

On Sunday I was up long before daylight, polishing and licking and patting for almost an hour. Something unheard of for me. Grandpa and Uncle Charlie didn't even tease me. They themselves were far too busy licking and polishing.

At last we were ready to go. We had decided the road was dry enough to take the motor car. I'd attempted to polish it up the day before, though it still bore the dents and scars of the accident.

We climbed in, I started up the Ford, and we headed down our long farm lane. I wouldn't be doing any speeding, even though I could hardly wait to get to town. Here and there along the road, mud holes waited for the unwary. And we sure didn't want mud stains on our carefully groomed Sunday suits and shoes.

We were there lots early, and I paced back and forth as I waited for Mary and her family to arrive.

Matilda came, though her leg was still in a walking cast. "I wouldn't have missed this day for the world!" she exclaimed and gave me one of her hurried, impulsive hugs. "I'm so happy for you, Josh," she bubbled. "Happy for both of you."

She welcomed Grandpa and Uncle Charlie with hugs as well. "Oh, I miss you," she cried. "All of you. The summer has seemed so long." There were tears in Matilda's eyes. "But I have good news," she hurried on. "I got the school I applied for near home."

"Ya mean yer not comin' back—?" began Grandpa.

"Oh, I couldn't," Matilda said softly. "I—I mean—I'm happy for Josh and Mary, but it wouldn't be the same now. I—mean—it wouldn't be fair to newlyweds to have someone—"

Grandpa nodded but I could see sadness in his eyes.

I had to admit that I hadn't even thought of Matilda's dilemma. But she was right. It would be better for Mary and me to get a good start on our own without an extra person around. It was going to be enough for us to share the house with Grandpa and Uncle Charlie. I would talk with Mary later about the new teacher, but as far as I was concerned it was just about time that one of the other neighbors took on boarding duty.

"But they've found a new teacher to replace me," Matilda's voice interrupted my thoughts, "and I've found a new school—so everything has turned out just fine."

At that point another interruption, and a welcome one—the Turleys arrived. Mary gave a squeal at the sight of Matilda and ran to meet her, her arms outstretched. They hugged and cried and hugged some more. I didn't mind. After all, Mary and I could look forward to a whole life together, beginning today. I just stood back and watched the goings-on.

Then I realized that I should be welcoming Mr. Turley. I had never seen him at church before, except of course for his wife's funeral. I shook his hand and smiled, not knowing exactly what to say. He gave a lopsided grin in return, looking a trifle uneasy. By then the girls had settled down, and Mary came over to me and slipped a warm little hand into mine. I whispered "Good morning, sweetheart," into her ear and made her blush prettily.

It was time for the service, so we all moved inside the church doors and found places to sit.

The service seemed unusually long. It was probably a very good sermon—Uncle Nat's always were. But for some reason I had a hard time concentrating on it. When I took a peek at the pocket watch I had gotten from Uncle Nat and Aunt Lou, I was astounded to discover it was even earlier than usual when the service was dismissed! Then I again felt Mary slip her hand in mine for just a moment, and I squeezed it gently in return. It was our little message to each other that it wouldn't be long until we'd be standing before the minister pledging our vows of love and commitment—and also that we were anxious for that moment.

Mary slipped away to Aunt Lou's as soon as she could, and I paced about checking to see that everything was in readiness. There certainly was no need—a lovely bouquet from Aunt Lou's garden graced the altar, and candles had been lit on either side. I straightened my tie—again—and smoothed back a wayward lock of hair.

At last Sally Grayson took her place at the organ and Uncle Nat stepped to the front of the church. That was my cue to join him. I gave Avery a bit of elbow and wiped my hands again on a handkerchief Aunt Lou had provided. I moved awkwardly forward down the aisle that looked as long as our farm lane. Boy, was I nervous. I tried to swallow but there was nothing there. Eventually Uncle Nat's reassuring smile came into focus, and I turned beside him along with Avery, cleared my throat and waited, trying hard to avoid all those eyes looking right at me.

Lilli came down the aisle next. She looked just fine. I'm guessing Avery noticed, too, for even in my mental fog I thought he was watching her progress rather carefully.

And then there was Mary, poised at the door on the arm of

her father, ready to take those few steps that would bring her down that aisle to me.

Her dress was simple but very appealing, and suited Mary perfectly. Her veil fell forward over her face, partly concealing her smile and her bright colored hair. But I could see her shining eyes, and they told me all I wanted to know.

"Dearly Beloved . . ." Uncle Nat's firm voice was an anchor for my whirling emotions. The ceremony was a short one—but I meant every word of the promises I made to Mary before God and many witnesses. From her expression and the directness of her answers, I knew she meant the promises to me as well.

"For richer, for poorer, in sickness and in health . . ." The words rang in my ears long after they were spoken.

But the words that really caught my attention were "to love and to cherish—till death us do part."

I had heard much about love. And I felt I understood it. I had no doubt in my mind about my love for Mary. But did I know what it meant to *cherish* her? Not much had been said in my presence about cherishing. I determined to do some looking into the meaning of that word at my first opportunity.

When the vows had been spoken, Uncle Nat indicated that I was to slip the wedding band on Mary's finger. And almost before I knew it he was pronouncing us man and wife. I lifted Mary's veil then to give her the expected kiss and could see fully the shine in her eyes and the flush to her cheeks. She was beautiful, my bride!

Uncle Nat presented us to the congregation. "Mr. and Mrs. Joshua Jones!" What a ring those words had! Mary and I looked at each other, and I felt an astonishment and excitement I'd never experienced before. I wished I could stop and kiss her again, but we had to go outside so folks could hug us and kiss us and give us their congratulations and throw rice and take pictures and all those usual things. I went through the whole thing in a daze. What a shame, too, because I wanted to always be able to look back with clear memories on this incredibly important day in my life.

We were finally ushered back into the church basement for the dinner. Guess folks were fairly hungry by then. For some reason I still hadn't felt hunger pangs. I went through all of the motions of eating, though, so Avery wouldn't rib me about being "lovesick."

Our friends gave little speeches and the Squire twins sang "Bless This House" and Matilda sang a lovely song based on a scripture text from the story of Ruth. Little Sarah played a piano piece. Lou said she'd worked hard on it all week. There were a few jokes here and there, and I guess they were funny—I mean, folks all laughed. All in all, the afternoon passed in fine style. Then we had gifts to open. In spite of the short wedding notice, the congregation did themselves proud. We got some real lovely things. Mary was thrilled over the linens, quilts, tea towels and such for our home, and that made me happy also.

At last people began to drift off to their homes, and finally it was just the family members who were left. I took off my suit coat and began to pack the gifts away in the car and help with the cleanup. Mary, still excited and happy, was also looking a bit tired.

We finally got everything cleared away or stacked in a corner. Then we slipped over to Aunt Lou's for a cup of hot tea and some slices of pumpkin bread. Mary took the opportunity to change from her wedding gown back into her Sunday dress, still looking like the pretty bride she was.

Mr. Turley excused himself as soon as Lilli and he had finished the light lunch. As he kissed Mary goodbye, he held her close. I saw tears in his eyes as he turned to go, and I wondered what it would be like to raise a daughter you loved so much only to give her over into the keeping of another man—particularly when her father had so recently lost his wife. I felt a pang of sympathy for Pa Turley. I followed him out to his team.

"Thank you, sir," I said sincerely, "for all you have done to make your daughter the beautiful person she is. I will love her always, I promise you."

Then we moved toward each other and I have never had such a bear hug. It suddenly hit me—*I have a pa! I mean, a real pa!* I hadn't had one of my own since I had been a small boy. I stepped back and looked at this man who now was a part of my life. I couldn't express all I was feeling. Instead I said, rather hoarsely, "How about comin' for supper—Wednesday night?"

He nodded his head and climbed into his wagon. "And Lilli, too, of course," I called after him. I watched him go until he turned the corner, and then I hurried in to tell Mary of my invitation to her pa—*our pa*—before I forgot.

It was late by the time we got home. We unpacked the car of the gifts and things Mary hadn't wanted to leave in town—things like her ma's silver tea service. We also had Mary's suitcases, although many of her belongings still waited in her downstairs bedroom, not having been moved back to her home after her accident.

There would be no honeymoon—at least not at the present. I was sorry about that. Mary and I had talked it over, and she had assured me she didn't mind. But still I felt she was a bit cheated out of what she rightfully deserved.

"After harvest," I'd promised her.

"Josh," she insisted, "the important thing is that we will be together, not *where* we will be together." I loved her even more for that.

As we carried Mary's personal things into the house, it became apparent that we menfolk, in all our hurrying and scurrying on short notice to prepare for the wedding, had given no thought to the room arrangements.

"Where should I put these?" Mary asked innocently.

"I—I—in—in my room, I guess," I began, but even as I said the words I knew that wouldn't work. I had the smallest room in the house. My tiny closet was already crowded with my few things. Mary's would never fit there too.

Grandpa cleared his throat. "The master bedroom," he said. "I'll git my things right outta there," and he moved to do just that.

"Oh, no," insisted Mary. "I wouldn't think of putting you out of your room, Grandpa."

A debate ensued, but Mary prevailed. It was finally decided that Mary and I would use Lou's old room. It was much roomier than mine and had a much larger closet. I carried Mary's things up to the room, and while she unpacked I busied myself making the evening coffee.

Mary was soon back down and took over in the kitchen. "Boy, is it ever good to have you back!" I teased.

"So you just wanted a cook!" she teased right back.

I looked around at Grandpa and Uncle Charlie. They both wore a very satisfied expression, and I figured that bringing Mary permanently into our family was about the smartest move I had ever made.

Chapter 15

Beginnings

WITH THE WEATHER TURNED for the better, our household back in order and my wife nearby, I got back to the haying again. Mary immediately took over her kitchen. My, how she did scrub and clean. I'm embarrassed to admit we menfolk had let things get even worse than I had realized.

She organized the rest of the house too—like moving the rest of my belongings from my old room to our new one, straightening the pantry, properly patching my worn overalls, sorting out the canning jars in the cellar and all sorts of other tasks. Every time I came in she was busy with something, though she often stopped to give me a hug and a kiss.

On Wednesday night the Turleys came for supper. Mary did herself proud, but then I guess her pa and Lilli were used to Mary's good cooking. I had to remind myself that Mary had likely cooked Pa Turley more meals than she had cooked for me.

Mary made life totally different for me when she was there.

I could hardly wait to get in from the field at night—and I'd always enjoyed field work. I looked toward the house a dozen times a day just to see if I could catch a glimpse of her. And she often slipped out with a drink of cold water or fresh buttermilk. She even came to the barn when I was milking and laughed as I squirted milk to the farm cat, chatting about her day, her plans for the house or garden while I did my chores.

Of course Grandpa and Uncle Charlie were awfully glad to have her back as well. Uncle Charlie seemed to walk a little jauntier, and Grandpa took to chuckling a good deal more. Though I was quite willing to share Mary's return with them, I marveled at the fact that she was really mine—just mine—in a very unique and special way. Every day the word "marriage" took on a new meaning for me, and I thanked God over and over for her and that He had thought of such a wonderful plan.

Friday night after all the chores had been done, the supper dishes washed and back in the cupboard, and we were gathered around the kitchen table enjoying various activities, I suddenly remembered my resolve to look up the word *cherish*.

My dictionary was up in my old room, I thought. But when I climbed the stairs to get it, I found that Mary had moved my few books as well. I went to Lou's room—I had to get that change made in my mind, to stop thinking of that room as Lou's—it was mine now, mine and Mary's. After rummaging around for a bit I found the dictionary. I flipped through the pages and came to the word.

"Cherish—to hold dear, to treat with tenderness, to nurse, nourish, nurture, foster, support, cultivate."

Wow! I read it again—and again. *I had promised before God to do all that!* I marveled. It had seemed to me that my loving Mary was sort of beyond my control. I mean, who could help but love Mary? But "cherish"—that was different. Most of the words in the definition were words of choice, of action—not feeling.

I knelt beside our bed with the dictionary open before me, and I went over each word in the list one at a time, promising God in a new way that with His help I would fulfill my promise to Him and to Mary. I even did some thinking on just how I might keep the promises. I prayed that God would help me to be a sensitive and open husband for Mary.

When I had finished my rather lengthy prayer, I heard a stirring at the door. It was Mary.

"I—I'm sorry, Josh. I didn't mean to interrupt. I—I—"

But I held my hand out to her.

"I want to show you something," I said, indicating the open book before me.

I rose to my feet and sat down on our bed. Mary crossed the room and sat beside me.

"Do you know what 'cherish' means?"

"Cherish?"

"Yeah. What we promised to do for each other last Sunday."

"Oh!" Mary exclaimed, her eyebrows lifting.

I traced the dictionary meaning of cherish while Mary read the words for herself. When she finished, her eyes met mine. We just looked at each other for a few minutes and then Mary spoke.

"Rather scary."

She was so serious, so solemn, that I began to laugh. I laid the dictionary on the bed beside me and reached for her. She snuggled into my arms and put her head against my shoulder, but I gently turned her face so that I could look directly into her eyes.

"Mary Jones," I said, enjoying the sound of her new name, "before God and with you as my witness, I promise to love you, to hold you dear, to treat you with tenderness, to nurse you, nourish you, nurture you, foster you, support you and cultivate your individuality—till death us do part."

I had needed to refer to the dictionary beside me a few times during my little speech, but I meant each word in a new way. When I finished there were tears in Mary's eyes.

"Oh, Josh," she murmured softly, "I love you so much."

That was really all I needed to hear.

I kissed her again.

"When you left the kitchen and didn't come back, I was a little worried," she admitted. "I thought—well, I don't really know what I thought."

"It took me awhile to find the dictionary," I confessed, "and then when I did, I needed some time to think it through and to pray for God's help."

I shifted so I could gather Mary more closely to me. The dictionary fell unheeded to the braided rug. I was through with it for the moment anyway.

"I need to go make the coffee," Mary murmured, but she didn't sound too convincing.

"Uncle Charlie knows how to make coffee," I reminded her.

"Yes—" But I stopped her protest with another kiss.

"We don't get much time alone," I reminded her. "I want you to tell me all the ways you can think of for me to keep the promises I've just made."

It was some time later that the smell of fresh-perked coffee drifted up the stairs and into our room, and Mary and I smiled at each other. It seemed that Uncle Charlie had found the coffeepot.

I finally finished the harvest. It wasn't a great crop, but it would get us through. The fall had been a dry one. In fact, the last moisture we got was what had come in July to delay my haying. I smiled every time I thought of that rain. It had speeded up my marriage to Mary, and for that I owed the rain a great deal.

We decided to further postpone our honeymoon. Mary said it was silly to spend the money when it might be needed elsewhere.

Mary got all her garden taken care of, and we settled in for another winter—one totally different for us, for now we had each other.

Matilda and Mary kept in touch by way of letters. Matilda's leg had mended well and she was enjoying her new school. There were even hints that some young man she had met was becoming rather special to her.

In November Lou gave birth to another girl, Patricia Lynn, her coloring darker than Sarah's. This little mite demanded a bit more attention than Sarah had as an infant. I looked at Lou with her family of four and wondered what it must be like. Certainly it meant work and sacrifice—but I figured it would be more than worth it.

With Matilda gone we had decided to subscribe to our own paper. I guess we had all become intrigued with the reading material that kept us informed of the world's events. Many evenings were spent sharing the paper around the kitchen table.

We were saddened and horrified by the news reports of the stock market crash. It seemed to be of great significance to many people—even causing suicides and such things. I couldn't understand how that whole financial world worked, though I did feel sorry for those who were directly affected by it all.

It sure didn't have much affect on our life, however. I mean, no one in our small community ever had money to invest in any stocks or such. The results of that crash would have little, if any, repercussions in our town, I reasoned. We were a bit relieved when the newspaper stopped screaming horrid headlines about the crash and went on to something else.

Winter came—according to the calendar—though the look of things didn't change much. There was no snow to speak of. The weeks trailed on, following one right after the other, and the world outside was just the same—brown and bare. Mary kept talking longingly about snow, and I must admit I was wishing for a good snowfall, too.

Christmas was nearing, though it was hard to get in the holiday spirit without a white world outside. But family members began to sneak around on their way to hide something somewhere. Secret whisperings and plottings made life rather interesting and fun. Then the whole house began to smell like a bake shop as Mary turned out special cakes and cookies. I wondered if we'd finish eating all those things even by Easter time.

Mary talked about trimmings for the tree, and I hoisted the boxes down from the attic and she went through them. I'd never realized before what a sorry lot they were. Mary set to work making new ones and even spent some of her egg money in town to replace several items. I could see that she received a good deal of pleasure out of making Christmas something special for all of us.

I looked forward to Christmas—but it sure would be nice to have some snow.

Chapter 16

Christmas

One little skiff of snow dusted the ground a few days before Christmas, and Mary got all excited over it. But it sure didn't last long. Before it had even covered the ground it began to melt off again. Mary was disappointed and I was disappointed for her. There wasn't anything I could do about snow for her Christmas, though.

"Josh," Mary said on the Saturday before Christmas, "we need to get a tree."

That was no problem. We had lots of small trees down along the crick that would look good with Christmas decorations.

"I'll get one," I promised.

"I thought maybe we could go together," offered Mary, and I grinned in appreciation.

"Great! When would you like to go?"

"Right after dinner—if that's okay with you."

"Fine."

And so the two of us headed out for the crick bottom right after the noon dishes were done.

It was colder than it had looked. I wondered if Mary might not be bundled up warmly enough, but I guess the vigorous walking helped keep her warm. Anyway, each time I asked her, she assured me that she was just fine.

The farm dog went along with us. Truth was, any time one of us went out, we didn't get far without Fritz at our heels. We didn't mind. It would have been fun to have Pixie along too, but she couldn't run very well anymore. She seemed to have arthritis like Uncle Charlie. Anyway, she didn't do any more walking than absolutely necessary. I even carried her upstairs each night. Most of her day was spent curled up in her little box behind the stove.

The pond in the pasture was frozen, and we took some time to slide back and forth. Sorta like being a kid again.

"We should have a skating party," enthused Mary, but I really didn't know who would want to come. All our old friends were either married with youngsters to care for or else had moved away.

For some reason I thought of Willie—maybe because he had skated with me on this very pond. Boy, I missed the guy. It still didn't seem real to me that he was gone—actually in heaven. I could see his face so plainly, could hear his banter and laughter—could sense his feel of mission and commitment when he spoke intensely of the needs of African villages for the gospel. Boy, I missed Willie.

I thought of Camellia. She had gone across the ocean to Willie's people now. I put money for her support in the collection plate the first Sunday of each month, and Uncle Nat forwarded it on to the Mission Society. We got an occasional prayer letter from Camellia, too. She loved Willie's Africans. She was kept busy with her nursing, for they were a poor people and many of them, old and young alike, had physical needs. Camellia was glad God had called her to this work. I still had a hard time picturing Camellia, the golden girl, trudging through destitute villages, visiting dirty, unkempt huts with medicines and love. But God did wonderful things with those who obeyed Him. Used people in ways we would have never dared suggest. Mary and I prayed daily for Camellia.

Mary brought my thoughts back to the present with a jerk when she lost her balance and ended up on her back in the middle of the ice. I was afraid she might have hurt herself, but she was laughing as I bent to help her and soon we were both down on the ice rolling and laughing.

It was fun until old Fritz jumped right into the middle of the fracas. He was barking and prancing and taking quick licks at our faces. By now Mary and I both decided we'd had enough, so we scrambled to our feet and started off again on our Christmas tree quest.

I'd figured it would be a quick, easy task. But with every tree I pointed out, Mary was sure we could do just a bit better. So on we walked, checking out tree after tree.

I was beginning to worry about getting home to do the choring when Mary at last found the very one she was looking for. It was about my height, with full, even branches.

"It will fit just fine in the parlor," Mary exclaimed and then added matter-of-factly, "Of course I will need to trim it up a bit."

I smiled wryly. She could trim it all she pleased just as long as we could cut the thing and get on home.

It wasn't hard to cut it down. It was a bit harder to get it home. There was no snow, so we couldn't drag it because Mary was afraid of damage to some of the branches—*probably the ones she'll eventually trim off anyway,* I thought but didn't say. That meant we had to carry it. Mary insisted on sharing in the effort. I lifted the big end and she took the small one, but carrying a tree, particularly one that has large, full branches and sways in the middle, is not an easy task.

We tripped about as much as we walked. The dog didn't help matters. He kept running around the tree and our feet, constantly getting in our way and tripping us up even more.

"Why don't *I* carry it?" I finally suggested.

"Oh, Josh. It's too heavy for one person."

I could have told her that it was too heavy for *two* people—but I didn't.

"I think it would be easier," I dared insist.

Mary looked reluctant. "Do you want it on your back—or your shoulder?" she finally conceded.

"My shoulder," I decided.

"I'll help you lift it up."

It didn't work very well that way either. Possibly it would have if Mary had allowed me to trim off some of the bottom branches—but she wanted the branches to come right down to the parlor floor. It was prettier that way, she said. So I was trying to carry a tree on my shoulder with branches right down to the bottom of the trunk. They poked me in the face and knocked off my hat.

I finally dumped the thing to the ground, and Mary gave a little gasp, fearful that I had broken some of her precious branches—which there were far too many of anyway.

"Look," I said, a little out of patience, "why don't I just get the team and wagon and come and haul it home?"

"Can you drive back in here with the team and wagon?" Mary wisely asked. I would have had to cut my way in and out again. There were no trails except those the cattle had made, and they were too narrow for a wagon to travel.

"Then I'll hook Barney to the stoneboat," I threw out, keeping my voice even.

Mary tipped her head slightly to consider it.

"It should work," she nodded in agreement. "You can sorta snake your way in and out among the trees."

I didn't like her description. "Snaking" didn't seem like much of a way for a man to travel.

"We need to put it someplace so you can remember where to find it," Mary continued, and I got even more huffed at that.

"I'll remember," I said flatly. "You think I'm an old man or somethin'?"

Mary looked a bit hurt by my response. "Of course not," she assured me apologetically; "but the trees all look alike an' *anyone* can forget."

She stressed the anyone.

"You forget that I was raised on this land," I reminded her loftily. "I know this crick bottom like the back of my hand. Roamed through here all my life—fishin' and huntin' cows."

Mary nodded but said nothing more.

We stashed the tree up against two anchored ones and started off for home. I checked the sky. The sun was already low on the horizon. I would need to hurry to get back for the tree before dark.

Mary reached out and slipped her mittened hand into mine, and I gave hers a bit of a squeeze. I wanted her to know I really wasn't mad at her or anything. We walked in silence for a while and then Mary began to chat about how she was going to decorate the tree and how pretty it would look. I could sense how special it was to her, and I was glad I hadn't insisted on lopping off some of the lower branches. "Nourish and nurture her" flashed through my mind, and I gave her hand another squeeze.

At home Mary went right on to the kitchen to get busy with supper, and I went to the barn to get old Barney.

It didn't take me long to get down to the crick bottom with the stoneboat, and I figured out how I'd slip right in, pick up that bulky tree and get back to the farmhouse in a jiffy.

I drove directly to where we had left it—but it wasn't there. Nor were the two trees we had braced it against. I couldn't believe my eyes. I started looking around, this way, that way, and the more I looked the more confused I got. I had to use the axe a few times to untangle the stoneboat from the brush, and that didn't make me so happy either.

All the time that I was searching, it was getting darker and darker. And I was getting madder and madder. I don't know why. It was my own dumb fault, but I was mad at Mary. I don't really know what she had done. Just been right, I guess. Anyway, I kept right on looking, too mad and too proud to give up. At the moment I couldn't think of anything more humiliating than showing up at home without that tree.

But in the end I had to give up. I was so confused I didn't even know which direction to point old Barney to get him back to the barn again. That made me even madder. Not being any snow, I didn't even have tracks to follow—though I was glad for that in a way. I sure wouldn't have wanted anybody to have followed my tracks through that brush. They'd have laughed at me for sure.

I finally conceded defeat and just gave Barney his head. He

weaved in and out—*snaked,* if you will—and finally came out into the open again. There across the field were the welcome lights of the farmhouse.

Mary ran to meet me as soon as I pulled into the yard. If she was disappointed about me not finding her tree, she didn't voice it.

"I was worried," she said instead.

"Too dark," I sorta growled. "I'll have to go pick it up later."

"Supper's ready," she told me. "Do you want to eat before you chore?"

I nodded—which she probably couldn't see considering how dark it was. Mary started back to the kitchen. "I've fed the pigs and chickens," she called over her shoulder, "and Grandpa carried the wood and water."

It should have made me feel great. Here I was coming in late without having accomplished my errand and chores still ahead of me, and I found them half done already. But it didn't make me feel great. It made me even madder. *Don't they think I can even do my own work?* I fumed.

I put Barney back in the barn and fed him. No soft words or appreciative pats for him tonight. I pushed a barn cat out of my way with a heavy-booted foot. He was lucky. I felt like kicking him.

On the way to the house it hit me. I was acting like a spoiled child, not a married man—and certainly not like a Christian husband who had promised to *love* and *cherish,* with all that it meant. Mary had done nothing to deserve my wrath. She was trying to make Christmas special. For me, for Grandpa, for Uncle Charlie. She had wanted a special tree. Had tried hard to help with the work of getting that tree. It wasn't her fault I couldn't find my way around my own woods.

But she had been right, she would likely—likely look at me with I-told-you-so in her eyes. *If she does—*

But I stopped right there beside the woodshed and prayed, reminding myself of all of my promises and asking God again to help me keep them. It didn't change my circumstances any, but it did make me a better supper companion.

The tree was not mentioned or the tree ornaments that sat waiting in the parlor either. Nor did Mary look at me as I had expected her to. She found something to busy herself with that Saturday evening and chatted away as if everything was just fine.

I loved her for it. It seemed that Mary was doing a much better job of keeping her promise to "cherish" than I was.

On Monday morning I hooked Barney up again. I still didn't know how I was ever going to find that tree, but I'd find it if I had to spend the whole day looking.

Then Mary complicated things. She came from the house, all bundled up, and smiled sweetly at me. "Thought I'd ride along," she stated in a matter-of-fact tone.

My head was spinning. *I'm going to be humiliated again.* I'd boasted of knowing my own crick bottom, of having a near-perfect memory. Both statements had proved to be false. I took a deep breath, gritted my teeth and directed Barney to head for the woods.

Halfway there I got this brilliant idea. I gave Mary a big grin and motioned for her to scoot up beside me.

"Wanna drive?" I asked her. Her face didn't brighten as I expected. For a moment I feared she might turn me down. Mary had her own little code of what rights belonged to the man of the family. But when I passed Barney's reins to her, she grinned and accepted them without further comment. I inwardly sighed with relief.

I was afraid as we neared the brush that she might pass the reins back to me. I had to do something to prevent that. I leaned over and lifted the axe to my lap.

"You drive," I said as casually as I could, "an' I'll cut any little shrubs that get in our way."

Mary just nodded.

We reached the woods, and she began to "snake" her way through with that stoneboat. Not once did she get hung up on anything, so I never got a chance to use that axe.

And would you believe it, she drove straight to that tree.

I made no comment as I loaded it. It filled up the stoneboat, so Mary and I had to walk back. She didn't seem to mind, and I sure didn't. On the way home she left the driving to me. I never even thought to share it. I was too busy wondering just how she had done what she had done. I mean, dead on! Right to where that tree stood waiting.

When we got back to the farmyard Mary went in to finish the washing. I put Barney away and went to do up a few odd jobs. I knew that in the evening we would be decorating the tree in the parlor. I looked forward to it now that we finally had the thing home.

We ran into another snag the next day. I didn't see it coming, though I should've been smart enough to sort it all out beforehand. You see, ever since Lou and Nat had married, we had always spent our Christmases with them. Lou had made the arrangements, cooked the dinner and everything. All we fellas ever did was show up.

Well, that's not quite true. We did our own shopping, wrapped our own gifts—in a manly sort of way—raised the turkey that we chopped the head off and plucked. But other than that, Lou took care of everything. I have no idea why I expected it to just remain that way.

Anyway, I should have been alerted when Mary said one morning as Christmas neared, "Do you mind if I invite Pa and Lilli for Christmas dinner?"

Of course I didn't mind. It sounded like a good idea to me, and Lou always cooked plenty of everything. We ate leftovers for days after Christmas was over.

So I heartily agreed to the arrangement. I even rode over to the Turleys and extended the invitation myself. I stayed awhile too. Just to chat with Pa Turley and to play a couple games of checkers. He didn't have much male companionship now that Mitch had left home, and I guess he missed it. Mary was happy when I returned with the news that they would be glad to come.

The next day Mary spoke about Christmas again. "I think you can bring in the gobbler now," she informed me. "I want to get it dressed and out of the way so everything won't need to be done at the last minute."

That made perfect sense to me. We men had always left it to the last minute simply because nothing else needed doing then for us. I had no idea what Mary's many tasks were going to be, but she was always powerful busy with something.

I killed the gobbler, plucked off the feathers and carried him to Mary's kitchen. She took over from there and soon he was ready to be hung outside in the shed where he would be kept frozen until needed further.

That night as we retired, Mary spoke again—and this time the truth of her Christmas plans finally got through to me. "Would you like to invite Nat and Lou?"

At first I couldn't understand the question at all.

"Invite—to what?" I asked innocently.

"For Christmas."

"We don't bother none with invitations," I said to Mary, tossing another sock in the corner. "We've done it so long now everybody just knows without invitations."

I figured in my ignorance that Mary had just reversed the order without meaning to.

But Mary hadn't reversed the order. She had known exactly what she said. "What do you mean?" she asked, stopping in the middle of pulling the pins from her hair.

"Well, I suppose the first few Christmases Lou invited us. After that—well, we just knew that every Christmas we would go there. Oh, not always 'there.' A few Christmases Lou's packed everything up and had the Christmas out here at the farm. But mostly, unless it's planned beforehand, we go on into town."

There was silence for a few minutes. Mary started to slowly unpin her hair again. "That was before you had a wife," she said softly.

I looked up then. Something in her voice was sending me funny messages.

"What do you mean?" I asked, wondering if I should have caught it already.

"That was before you had a wife," she repeated slowly as though I was dense or something.

"What does that have to do with it?" I dared ask.

Mary's voice raised a bit and she answered rather quickly, "It has a good deal to do with it, I should think."

"It hasn't changed the fact that we are still family—that Lou—"

But Mary swung to face me and I could see a stubborn set to her chin and a hurt look in her eyes. I didn't get any further. At least not just then.

The silence hung heavy again.

Finally Mary broke it. She fought to keep her voice controlled—even.

"Josh," she ventured, "what do you think has been goin' on around here for the past several days?"

I shrugged. I couldn't follow her.

"The bakin'? The plannin'? The tree? The turkey?" Mary went on.

I shrugged again. I had the feeling that no matter what I said I was going to be in trouble.

"Christmas, Josh. Christmas," Mary said with emphasis. "I have been gettin' ready for our first Christmas. Now, if I wasn't going to be allowed to *have* Christmas—why've I been allowed to *prepare* for it?"

"It's—it's not that you aren't allowed," I stammered.

Mary ran a brush through her hair. "Good," she said simply. "Then we will have Christmas as planned. Do you want to invite Nat and Lou?"

Oh, boy! Talk about not communicating. We were running full circle.

I stood to my feet and crossed to stand in front of her. Somehow I had to get things cleared up.

"Mary," I said in exasperation, "we always—Grandpa,

Uncle Charlie and me—go to Aunt Lou's each Christmas. Every year. We—"

But Mary had turned her back on me. It made me angry. I wanted to reach out and turn her around again. Make her face me.

"That was before," she insisted.

"Before? What does that have to do with it? Before! It doesn't change Christmas. We are all *still* family. Families are to be together at Christmas. Not just—just little chunks of them. All of them. Can't you see? Don't you understand?"

Mary wheeled around then. There were tears spilling down her cheeks. "No," she stated with a sob, "*you* don't see. I've worked for days, Josh, no—*weeks*, to get ready for this first Christmas. Always before I've had to leave you at Christmas and go home to my family. Well, now *we* are family, Josh. You and me. I wanted this Christmas to be ours. To be special. I thought you wanted it, too," she sobbed. "But now—now you say that Christmas is to be a trip to town—to Lou's to have dinner together. Well, I care about the family as much as you do, Josh. I love Lou and Nat—and the kids—but that's—that's not the way I had planned our first Christmas."

Mary was crying hard by the time she finished her speech. I found myself wondering if Grandpa and Uncle Charlie were hearing every word. The walls certainly were not soundproof. Well, let them hear. This was our business.

I tried one more time.

"It's not that I don't want our Christmas to be special," I argued. "To me it is always special to be with Nat and Lou."

Mary reached for a corner of her nightgown and wiped away her tears. She didn't cry any further, and I thought I had won. That she had finally listened to reason.

She didn't say "very well," or "fine," or anything like that. In fact, she didn't say anything at all. She just laid her brush back down on the dresser and walked around the bed to slip into her side. She even allowed the customary good-night kiss after I had put out the light.

It was some time in the middle of the night that I awakened. I had the feeling that I'd heard something, but as I lay there in the darkness, straining to hear whatever it had been, there was total silence. And then it came again. Just a shaky little sob from Mary's side of the bed.

I rolled over then and reached out a hand to her.

"Mary?" I questioned in a whisper. "Mary, is something wrong?"

"Oh, Josh," she sobbed, slipping her arms about me. "I'm so sorry. I shouldn't have—shouldn't have been so insensitive. I—"

"What are you talking—?" I began, not understanding, completely forgetting our little tiff at bedtime.

"Of course you want to be with your family, like always. I'm sorry that I—"

So that was it.

I held Mary and let her cry. All the time I thought on what had transpired. For the first time I began to see and understand Mary's thinking. We were family now—Mary and I, and with the years we might be blessed enough to have other family members join us. We had the right and the responsibility to make our own traditions—our own Christmases. Sure, the rest of the family would always be dear to us—and we could share and be with them—but not *lean* on them. Not depend on their traditions anymore.

My hand patted Mary's shoulder, and I lay staring into the dark thinking and praying a bit, too.

I had slipped again. I had failed in cherishing Mary. I had not been sensitive to her needs, had not nurtured nor supported her. Would I ever learn?

"Mary," I whispered against her hair, "you were right and I was wrong. I'm sorry. Truly sorry."

There was silence again. I dared to continue.

"We should have our own Christmases. *We* are family. It's important to—to both of us."

Mary tipped her face in the blackness. "It's all right," she said. "I don't mind. Really."

But I wasn't turning back now. "I'll go see Aunt Lou tomorrow," I informed Mary. "Grandpa and Uncle Charlie can still go. We'll have Lillie and Pa here."

"No," said Mary. "We'd be splitting up family. That wouldn't be right."

"I'll talk to Lou," I insisted. "She'll understand."

"*I'll* talk to Lou," said Mary. "We'll work it out."

"But—" I began. Mary reached one finger out in the darkness and placed it on my lips.

"Trust me?" she asked simply and I nodded my head against her finger to assure her that I did.

Chapter 17

Adjustments

GRANDPA DROVE MARY IN to see Lou the next day. He was looking for an excuse to go into town anyway. I figured he had some more Christmas shopping to do.

Everything worked out just fine. It was decided that Christmas would be at our house with Uncle Nat, Aunt Lou and family, Pa Turley and Lilli, all around our table. Mary would take care of all the arrangements for the dinner. Grandpa confided to me that he felt Lou was a bit relieved. The new baby was still keeping her up nights a good deal.

Lou and Mary also agreed that in the future each would take turns having Christmas dinner. That sounded like a sensible arrangement to me. It gave both women a Christmas "off" and yet allowed each to have Christmas just her way on the Christmas when it was her turn.

I was proud of Mary. She had been sensitive and caring—and yet had shouldered her share of family responsibility.

That Christmas turned out to be the best I had celebrated up to that point in my life. Mary did a fine job with the dinner—just like I'd known she would. The turkey was cooked to perfection, the potatoes fluffy and the gravy as smooth as silk. All the good things she had been baking over the previous days appeared on the kitchen sideboard—right along with the honored silver tea set from which she served the tea and coffee.

The weather was fine—though we never did get our Christmas snow, nor any other snow, for that matter. The families arrived early and left late, and we all had a great time together.

Of course Lou's four little ones added a lot of spark to the occasion. Sarah was too grown-up now to be relegated to the children's status. Jonathan too had matured a lot over the summer months and wasn't nearly as hard to keep track of, but Timmy more than made up for him. Someone had to watch the boy every minute. I finally had to carry Pixie up to the bedroom and shut the door on her. Timmy insisted on petting her and holding her, and poor old Pixie's bones were too fragile for Timmy's kind of handling. He tried to be careful, but being a small boy he was pretty awkward at showing his affection.

Baby Patty slept a good share of the day. Aunt Lou ruefully commented that it might mean a long, wakeful night. I had no idea what that was like and wasn't particularly interested in finding out.

Pa Turley really seemed to enjoy being with the family. He watched the antics of the children with loud guffaws and slaps to his knees. I couldn't help but wonder, *What'll he think of having grandchildren of his own?*—though I felt I knew.

Lilli was quiet. She helped Mary in the kitchen, but her mind didn't seem to be on it much. I wasn't too surprised when along about midafternoon Avery appeared at our door. I invited him in, but he declined. Said he'd come to take Lilli for a bit of a drive. We teased them some, but they just flushed and bundled up to get away from all of us.

When they returned Avery accepted our invitation to share leftover turkey and homemade buns. We formed a little four-some and played dominoes. Mary and I won, hands down, but I don't think our opponents were doing too much concentrating on the game. Avery and Lilli were the last to leave that evening.

We were all tired but happy when we retired. Mary and I cuddled close in Aunt Lou's old bed and talked over each of the day's happenings. It was fun to go over it all again.

"You know which gift I liked the very best?" Mary asked me.

"Which?"

"The mirror. The new mirror."

I wasn't really surprised. I'd noticed her stretching or stooping, trying to see herself in Lou's old mirror. The gilt was wearing off at just the wrong place.

"What was your favorite?" asked Mary.

"Oh, boy! That's tough. I liked them all."

But Mary wasn't to be put off so easily.

"Come on, Josh. Favorite."

I reviewed the gifts Mary had given to me. "I guess the pullover sweater," I said after much thought.

"The sweater?"

"And do you know why? Because you made it yourself. For me." I paused a moment and then went on with a chuckle, "And you know why else?"

"*Why* else?" teased Mary. "Is that proper English?"

"Of course it is. *Why* else would I say it?" I bantered back and Mary gave me a little jab in the ribs.

"Okay—so *why* else?" she asked me.

"Because it actually fits," I laughed. "It has two arms—and they are the same length. It has a hole up top for my head and one at the bottom for my waist."

By now Mary was chuckling too but she gave me another playful jab. "Are you saying you didn't think I could knit?" she accused me.

"No," I answered, dodging away from another jab, "but I have seen a few sweaters in my day that were made by girlfriends or new brides. You had to ask to be sure what the thing was."

Mary gave me one more jab. That one I figured I deserved.

On a cold, windy day near the middle of the month, I came in one morning to find Mary in tears. I couldn't think of anything I had done, and I was sure Grandpa or Uncle Charlie wouldn't do anything to make her weep. For a moment I feared Mary might be ill, and that scared me something awful.

I didn't ask questions. I didn't have time. Mary threw herself into my arms and sobbed against my shoulder. By now I was really worried. My eyes traveled to meet Grandpa's across the room, but he wouldn't look at me. He was busy staring out of the window at the bleak, sunless day. Uncle Charlie was nowhere to be seen.

In my mind I frantically reviewed family members, wondering if bad news had come in some way while I'd been out. But I hadn't heard a horse, and the farm dog had been with me all the time. His ears were sharper than mine, and he most certainly would have heard if someone had come.

"Sh-h-h. Sh-h-h," I tried to quiet Mary, brushing aside strands of fine hair from her tear-streaked face.

"Sh-h-h. Tell me. Tell me what's wrong."

Mary swallowed hard and tried to get control. "It's Pixie," she finally managed to gasp out. "I found her in her box behind the stove."

"Pixie?"

Mary burst into fresh tears and clutched me even more tightly.

I wanted to free myself and check on Pixie. The little dog might be in need of some attention. But I couldn't just leave Mary. Not the way she was feeling now. I held her more tightly and rubbed her shoulder and patted her back.

When her tears finally subsided, I put her gently from me and went to kneel beside the stove to check on Pixie. It was far worse than I had feared, and my whole being rushed to deny it. The little body was lifeless. There was nothing I could have done. She was already stiff and cold.

Tears came to my own eyes. I picked her up as gently as I could and ran my hands again over the silky sides and let my fingers toy with the floppy little ears. *She's been a good dog—a good friend,* I mourned. Pixie had been with me ever since my dearly loved Gramps had found her for me so many years ago. Boy, would I miss her. It reminded me of how much I missed Gramps.

I knew Pixie was old, that she had been stiff and arthritic and in pain much of the time. She was far better off having just slept her way out of life. But I still fought against the reality of it. If I'd had the power right then, I'd have brought her back.

I didn't have that power, so all I could do was hold her up against my chest. The small body sure didn't feel like it usually did. I was used to her little tail wagging gently as I petted. I was used to a little lick with a pink tongue every now and then. I was used to warmth and energy. And now there was only the quiet, stiff, lifeless little form. I felt almost repelled by it—but I couldn't put her down. I just kept running my hand over her, speaking to her as though I thought she should awaken.

Mary came to where I knelt and laid a hand on my head, running her fingers softly through my hair.

"I'll fix a box," she said quietly.

For a moment I wanted to protest. Pixie had been *my* dog. I would fix the box. And then I remembered how much Mary had loved her too and I nodded in agreement, the tears flowing again.

I pulled Pixie's small bed out from behind the stove and laid her gently back down. Without a backward glance I arose, pulled my heavy mittens back on and left the kitchen.

I found the shovel and a pick and chose a spot in the garden. I wanted her to be down under the trees beside the grave of my first little pup, the one I had named Patches. *Gramps brought me that puppy too,* I remembered as I raised the pick above the frozen ground. It was hard digging. Maybe that was good. I needed something difficult to concentrate on for the moment. I put my full strength behind each swing of the pick. Then I shoveled out the frozen clumps of dirt, making a hole big enough to hold a small box. A small box with an even smaller dog.

Tears froze on my cheeks as I worked. *She might've been small,* I thought, *but she was all heart.* All heart and love. I'd never known anyone who had loved me like my small dog had. She asked no questions, demanded no apologies. She just loved me—Josh Jones—just as I was.

I guess I got a little carried away on the size of the hole. I made it bigger than it needed to be, but perhaps I wasn't ready to go back to the house yet. I needed a little more time to be alone. With Pixie's death went my last visible memory of Gramps.

Oh, I had lots of memories. Things that I treasured as I pulled them out and thought on them—which I did often. But with Pixie those memories had been different, more vivid. Each time I picked up the little dog I could see the age-softened hands of Gramps as he handed her to me for the first time.

I remembered Aunt Lou sharing with me how Gramps had walked into town after my first puppy was killed and searched the town streets until he had found me another puppy. I remembered too how small Pixie was, and how Gramps had told me that she would need special care and love.

Pixie had been my little love-gift, that's what she had been. It was Gramps special love for me that prompted the giving, and it was Pixie's and my special love for each other that had helped us share so many things over the years.

And now she's gone. I had known all along that one day it would happen, but I had just kept pretending in my heart that I could hold it off somehow.

I finally stopped my digging, wiped the frozen tears from my cheeks and went to put away the pick. I would still need the shovel.

Mary had the box all ready. She had lined it with some soft material that made Pixie look as though she were all cuddled in and snug as she liked to be. The lid was next to it, and I knew Mary expected me to put that in place after I'd told my little dog goodbye one last time.

I ran my hand over the silken fur and then placed the lid on the box. I pulled on my heavy mitts and looked at Mary.

She had wiped away all her tears, but I could still see the sadness in her face.

"I thought you might like to be alone," she said softly to explain why she didn't have her coat on. I nodded, surprised that she knew me so well so soon, and then I picked up the little box and went back to the garden.

After I had completed my sorrowful task, I stayed outside for a while finding little chores I could do. Mary didn't come looking for me. When I finally decided I was ready to face the family and go on with life, I went back to the kitchen. I could smell the coffee brewing even before I opened the door, and I realized just how chilled I was.

Mary's eyes met mine and we spoke to each other even without words. She smiled then, just a tiny little one, and I gave her a bit of a nod.

Uncle Charlie reappeared. We tried to talk normally at the table. Didn't seem much to talk about, save the weather. It worked for a time. By then I had thawed out a bit and was feeling some better, though I knew it would be a long, long time until I got over my hurt. Mary knew it too. I could feel her love and understanding even when a whole room separated us. It was a marvel, this being man and wife. I began to wonder how I had ever functioned before Mary had changed my whole life. I hoped and prayed I would never need to function without her again.

For the first time in my life I began to realize what Grandpa had suffered over the years without Grandma—and why Gramps had commented to me about being anxious to get to heaven. It gave me a new respect and sympathy. And I think it opened up a whole new understanding of the word *love* for me too.

Chapter 18

Life Goes On

I CAME IN FROM the morning chores expecting breakfast on the table as usual. It was—after a fashion. The pot of rolled oats still simmered on the stove, the coffee bubbled in the coffeepot. Thick-sliced bread was toasted, the table set, but it didn't take sharp eyes to know that something was amiss.

"Where's Mary?" I asked Uncle Charlie, who gave the lumpy porridge another stir while Grandpa poured the coffee.

"She's not feeling well," Uncle Charlie informed me and went on quickly when he saw the look in my eyes. "Nothin' serious. Jest a tummy upset, she said. Bit of the flu, I 'spect."

I didn't even wait to remove my outside wraps but headed for the stairs.

Mary was lying on the bed in her clothes, so I knew she had been up.

"I'll be fine," she assured me wanly. "Just—"

I'd already heard that little speech from Uncle Charlie. I sat on the bed and laid a hand on her forehead.

"I don't have a fever, Josh," Mary protested. "I already checked it myself."

"You feel hot to me," I argued.

"As cold as your hand is from chorin', anything that isn't freezing would feel hot," Mary reminded me. "Go on," she prompted. "Go have your breakfast."

"Aren't you going to eat?"

"It would be pointless," insisted Mary. "I'd just bring it right back up again."

"Could I bring—"

"Josh," said Mary with a bit of impatience, "I can't even stand the *smell* of it."

I tucked a blanket about her and left her then, though I was still worried even with her assurances that she'd be up soon.

True to her word, Mary came down later. She still looked pale, but she insisted that she felt just fine. She proved it by taking over her kitchen chores.

For the next three mornings the scene was repeated. I was getting kind of tired of Uncle Charlie's version of our breakfast porridge—even though I'd eaten it most of my life. I was also getting very concerned about Mary. One morning she didn't make an appearance until almost noon, and even then she looked as if she should be back in bed. I tried to talk her into staying in for the day so she could lick this thing, whatever it was. But who was I to argue with a woman who's made up her mind?

When it happened the fifth morning in a row, I decided something must be done. Without saying anything to Mary, I saddled Chester and headed off to town. I figured it was about time Doc was consulted about the matter.

Doc arrived at the farm soon after I had returned home again. By then Mary was up and about. She looked pale and often turned her face away when she lifted the lid to stir a pot, as though she couldn't bear the sight or smell of whatever she was cooking.

Mary looked surprised when I ushered Doc into the kitchen. Then she set about putting on the coffeepot, probably assuming that he had just popped in to warm up on his return from a neighborhood call. Doc was content to wait, visiting with Grandpa and Uncle Charlie, but I could see that he was watching Mary carefully out of the corner of his eye.

"Hear you haven't been feeling so well, young lady," Doc said as he stirred in some cream into his cup.

"A bit of a flu bug, I guess," Mary answered off-handedly as she passed him a plate of cookies.

"Maybe," agreed Doc. "It sure is making the rounds again. But Josh thought I should check it out, just in case."

All eyes turned to me. I was especially aware of Mary's.

"It's not always flu when the stomach acts up," Doc went on. "Josh is right," he said in answer to Mary's expression. "No harm in checking."

After we had finished our coffee, Doc sent Mary up to our room to prepare for the examination.

"Do—do you think it's serious?" I ventured before Doc went up to join her.

He put his hand on my shoulder as he rose. "No point in worrying about it till you have something to worry about, Josh," he said, while Grandpa and Uncle Charlie nodded solemnly in agreement.

He wasn't gone long. When he appeared in the doorway I was all ready for the explanation of Mary's illness. I started to ask but Doc stopped me. "Mary is waiting for you," he told me, and I felt my heart constrict with fear. I ran up the stairs two at a time and flung the door open.

Mary was propped up on two pillows. Instead of pale, now her cheeks were a trifle flushed and—I crossed quickly to her after swinging the door closed behind me. I wanted privacy if I had to hear the worst.

"Sit down, Josh," Mary said gently. I did so and took her hand in mine.

"Is it—? Are you really sick?" I managed.

"No," Mary answered and her eyes were shining. "I'm just fine."

"Then—then—?"

Mary began to smile, then giggle. Here I was about to die of worry and she sat there giggling like a silly schoolgirl.

"Josh," she began, and took a deep breath to try to calm herself. She seemed about to explode with excitement. "How would you like—like to be a father?"

"I'd like it," I stammered. "You know I would. We've talked about it—"

"Good," squealed Mary, "because you are going to be one!"

Her words didn't make much sense, but the way she was pulling on my arm and beaming made me realize that something good was happening—something extraordinary. I started sorting through the conversation again, looking for the answer and finally it got through to me.

"You mean—now?" I yelled back, grabbing her by both shoulders.

"Well—well—" she teased, but I had already jumped up from the bed. I ran down the hall and bounded down the stairs two or three at a time. "We're gonna have a baby!" I shouted to Grandpa and Uncle Charlie, who were both on their feet and hollering along with me before I could make full circle. Then I ran back up the stairs again and grabbed Mary. I held her close and we laughed and rejoiced together.

I finally stopped rocking her back and forth and held her at arms' length. "You didn't know—?" I questioned, gazing into her face. Somehow I thought that women automatically knew these things.

"I suspected," she admitted, "but I still wasn't sure."

"When?" was my next question.

Mary screwed up her face. "The timing's not great," she said slowly. "The baby will arrive right in the middle of harvest."

"We'll manage fine," I quickly assured her. "We'll find you some help."

"So this is why you've been feelin' sick?" I went on.

She nodded.

"I don't remember Lou being sick like that. It scared me," I admitted.

"Some women are. Some women aren't," Mary explained matter-of-factly. "Anyway, it shouldn't last for long, Doc said."

But Doc was wrong. Mary continued to feel sick for many weeks. Months, in fact. She lost weight and looked pale and fragile. It tore me apart to hear her in the mornings. I felt responsible for the way she was feeling and I sure would have gladly taken her place.

We menfolk took turns cooking breakfast. I even hung a blanket over Mary's door so the odors from the kitchen wouldn't bother her as much. Other than that, it seemed we simply had to wait it out.

In March we had a visit from Lilli and Pa Turley. They brought both good and bad news. Lilli brought the good news. Bubbling as she shared it, she told us that Avery had asked her to marry him and she had said yes. The wedding was set for June.

Pa's news brought sadness to Mary's eyes.

"I've decided to put the farm up for sale," he informed us.

I saw Mary start and wondered what thoughts were going through her mind. She didn't speak them then; she simply nodded.

"I've given it a lot of thought," went on Pa Turley. "Mitch isn't interested in farmin'. He has him a good job in the city now." Pa Turley sat twisting his coffee cup this way and that as he looked into the steaming interior. "Don't 'spect he'll ever return home to the land . . ." His voice trailed off.

"Never was no good at batchin'," he mused after a moment of silence.

"What will you do?" Mary finally found voice to ask. My thoughts had already jumped ahead, and I was about to call Mary aside to suggest that we offer Pa the downstairs bedroom.

"Emma—yer aunt Emma over to Concord—has been after me fer some time to move in with her. She'd like someone about the house to keep things in order like—an' she knows I don't wanna be alone. She thinks thet it would work best fer both of us."

"And what do you think?" Mary asked calmly.

"I've no objections," Pa Turley answered a bit quickly. "Always got along with Emma the best of any of my sisters."

Mary looked at me and I nodded. She took a big breath as though in relief, her eyes thanking me as she said, "You're welcome here, Pa."

Pa Turley pushed back his chair and waved the offer aside in one quick motion. "Oh, I couldn't," he protested.

"And why not?" questioned Mary. "We've got the room. We'd be glad to have you, wouldn't we, Josh?"

"Sure would," I assured him. "A room right there," I said, pointing to the downstairs bedroom, "or one right up there at the head of the stairs. Take your pick."

Pa Turley seemed to be having a mental debate. He finally sighed deeply and pulled his chair closer to the table and his cup.

"Much obliged," he said with feeling. "Guess it's always good to know thet yer wanted. But—I think thet we'd best leave things be. I—I would be welcome here. I know thet. But Emma—Emma needs me. There's a difference there, ya know? No, I think thet we'd best let things be as planned."

Mary and I looked at each other, and we knew that we had to let him decide the matter. "Well, as long as you know you're more than welcome, Pa," I told him.

"You'll visit?" asked Mary.

"Oh, why sure," he promised. "Got three girls all a'livin' here. 'Course I'll visit. 'Sides, I sure wanna keep up on the grandchildren."

Mary and her pa smiled fondly at each other.

That night Mary and I lay in our bed talking over the day's events. I decided to tell her what had been churning through my mind ever since the Turleys' visit.

"I've been thinkin'," I said softly into the dark, "I'd like to buy Pa's land."

I felt Mary move slightly in order to see my face. It was too dark in the room, so she settled back in her spot beside me.

"You need more land, Josh?" she asked.

"Not—not really. Not right now. But—but it was your home, your family's land for as long as I can remember—as long as *you* can remember. I thought—I thought it might be hard—that you might sorta like to keep it."

There was silence and then Mary said softly into the night, with a break in her voice, "Thank you, Josh."

I ran my hand over her soft hair and traced the scar over her eye with one finger. "Besides," I went on slowly, "who knows? Maybe we'll have a son and he'll need the land. I'd be pleased to give him his grandpa's farm to work."

Mary chuckled at the thought and put her head on my shoulder. "If you can—if you can work it out, Josh, I'd be most happy about it," she whispered, and a sob caught in her throat. "It would only seem right, wouldn't it—and it would make Papa so happy."

I decided on a trip to town the very next day to see what arrangements could be made.

The banker was agreeable, and Pa Turley sure was. It took some time to get all the paperwork sorted out and processed. But in the end the Turley farm belonged to the Joneses. Pa acted like a heavy burden had been lifted from his shoulders when I handed him the check for the farm. He couldn't say anything. He just reached out and gave me a big bear hug, and I knew he felt that he wasn't really giving up the land—just handing it on to his family.

He had a farm sale then and packed his few belongings for moving on to his sister's. Lilli went to live with Faye to await her wedding to Avery.

Mary and I drove Pa into town to catch the train for Concord.

He'd already said goodbye to his other two daughters. He didn't have much to say on the way, but his eyes sure did study out every farm and field as we traveled along. *It's like he's closing the door on his past life,* I thought, *and getting ready to open a new one.*

When we got into town he excused himself and said he'd like to take a bit of a walk before the train pulled in. Mary had groceries to purchase and I had some harness parts to pick up, so we let him off and promised we'd be there at the station when the train arrived.

I wondered what the little walk was about. Figured he might have some old friends he wanted to say goodbye to or something—and then I saw him head off in the direction of the cemetery.

He was going to say his goodbye to Mrs. Turley. Guess he missed her far more than any of us knew. More than he'd ever miss the farm. Maybe sister Emma would be good for him—though of course I knew she'd never take the place of the one he had shared life with for so many years.

Like we'd said, Mary and I were both there when the train pulled in. 'Course the tears flowed some with the goodbyes. I knew it was hard for Mary, but she was brave about it. And then the train was pulling off and we were alone on the platform, the wind whipping Mary's coat about her small form. I took her hand and led her from the station. More than ever, she was mine to care for now. She had neither ma nor pa to lean on when she needed them. I was really all she had.

Chapter 19

Happiness

WITH THE ADDITION OF the Turley farm, I had even more fields to plant that spring. I knew Pa Turley had been a good farmer in his day, but perhaps he'd sorta lost heart since the death of Mrs. Turley. Anyway, there was a lot of catching up to do in working up the land.

Mary was patient about my long, long days. Many times I saw her only at breakfast and for a few minutes at supper before I fell into bed exhausted. She didn't make many trips to the fields, either, with refreshments as she had usually done. Partly because it was more difficult for her with the baby coming, but mostly because some of the new fields I worked were so far away. Instead, she packed a lunch for me each morning.

We didn't get much rain at all that spring, so I wasn't slowed down any with the planting. In fact, it was so dry that neighboring farmers were all talking about it and wondering if the seed would have enough moisture to sprout.

The crash of the faraway stock market did affect us. I guess it affected the whole world. Everyone sorta held their breath, waiting to see just what calamity would strike next. I prayed that there wouldn't be one and that I would be able to take care of the family members who were my responsibility.

Lilli married in June as planned. Pa Turley came back for the wedding and spent a few nights with us before returning to Aunt Emma. Mary was so glad to see him. While he was there, he and Grandpa and Uncle Charlie all worked on a cradle together. They seemed to take great pleasure in the project, and Mary of course was thrilled.

The grain did start to grow. Here and there green shoots began to poke their heads through the soil, and I felt more relaxed. With a good rain I was sure we'd be well on our way. But the rains still didn't come, and pretty soon the small spears began to turn kind of yellow and wilt in the sun. I guess I should have faced the facts then, but I still kept hoping that with a good rain the grain could pick up again.

The summer was a hot one too. I felt sorry for Mary, being heavy with child as she was. The heat was especially hard on her. But she didn't complain. Just slowed down with the many jobs she had. Without rain her garden wasn't looking near as good as it normally did, and that bothered her. She and Grandpa carried pails of water to some of the plants, but it was too much work to try to water the whole garden.

When haying time came, the crop was thin and stunted. I worried about how we'd make it through the winter for feed as I put what hay we had up into stacks. Wasn't near as much as most years.

I guess the thing that kept me going that summer, the knowledge that brought excitement to both Mary and me, was the anticipation of the arrival of our child. The whole family was waiting for the baby, and now that Mary had gotten over her morning sickness and seemed to be feeling fine except for the heat, we were all sorta counting the days.

What harvest there was that year was so thin and runty, I wondered if it really merited cutting—but like all the farmers around me I went to work in the fields anyway. Lilli came to help Mary. It sure was decent of Avery to allow her to come, them being newlyweds and all. Mary was grateful for the help, and she and Lilli seemed to get along real good in the kitchen together. They didn't even need to talk about certain things—seemed to just understand what each one was supposed to do without saying so.

While Lilli was there, most of the canning was done. I had our little bit of grain ready for the threshing crew. Mary was hoping we'd get the crew out of the way before our little one decided to join the family. For her sake, I was hoping so too.

Mary and I talked a lot about our coming baby. Of course we talked "boy or girl." I told Mary I'd be happy with either one—but I think she knew I figured a son would be pretty nice. I mean, I had this extra farmland and all, and I sure did hope that someday a son would be farming it. *But a girl would be nice, too,* I decided as I thought of Sarah and little Patricia. Patty was walking now. She was over her fussiness and was a cuddly, lovable, contented little darling. I didn't mind the thought of a daughter one little bit.

The threshing crew had just moved in and set up, and the first load of bundles had been placed on the conveyer belt, when I glanced toward the house and saw Lilli standing in the yard waving her apron back and forth like the house was on fire. For a moment I couldn't understand her action, and then I realized the waving was meant to get my attention. Even so it took a while for me to understand what Lilli was trying to tell me.

"Go ahead, Josh. I'll take over here," said a voice beside me, and I turned to see Avery also watching the waving apron.

Then I understood what it was all about. It was Mary. *It must be time* . . . I dropped the pitchfork right where I was standing and took off for the farmyard on the run. Lilli saw me coming and turned to hurry back into the house.

Puffing from the run, my chest heaving and my lungs hurting, I just looked, wild-eyed, around the little circle in the kitchen, hoping that someone would give me information.

Lilli was stoking the fire and putting the kettle on. Her back was to me but she spoke anyway—evenly, controlled, just as though nothing out of the ordinary was happening.

"It's time to fetch Doc, Josh."

I headed for the stairs. I had to see Mary first.

She was lying in our bed, her face damp with perspiration, her hair scattered across the pillow. When she saw me she managed a weak smile, but I could see relief there too.

"It's time, Josh," she whispered.

I went to the bed, knelt beside it and took her hand. For a moment I couldn't speak. I pressed her fingers to my lips. She reached out and gently brushed at my cheek.

Before I could even tell her that I would hurry, her hand tightened on mine and she squeezed my fingers until they actually hurt. Her face drained of all color and her breath caught in a ragged little gasp.

It scared me half to death. I was sure something was dreadfully wrong. And then she began to relax again. I could feel the tension on my fingers lessening, and Mary let her head roll back on the pillow so that she could look at me again.

"Go, Josh," she whispered. "You'd best hurry."

I nodded and was gone.

I hadn't been using the Ford much, but I ran directly to it now. I prayed that it had enough fuel to get me to town and back. I also prayed that it would start right off after sitting for most of the summer.

It did start. I thanked God all of the way down the lane, and then I wheeled onto the road and headed for town just as fast as I could push that thing.

Doc wasn't home. I nearly panicked. Thanks to his wife, I found him in the barber shop getting his monthly haircut.

"It's Mary!" I gasped out. You would have thought I had run all the way to town. "Mary needs you. Now."

Doc didn't fool around any. He jerked the white cloth from around his neck.

"I'll be back, Charlie," he flung over his shoulder and left with only half a cut. Then we were off for his house to pick up his bag and whatever else he needed.

The trip home was a fast one. I turned once to look at Doc to see if I was scaring the living daylights out of him, but he was grinning just a bit as he held on to his hat, and I got the feeling he was actually enjoying the ride.

We wheeled into the yard and screeched to a stop right before the picket fence. Doc grabbed his bag and headed for the house. I wasn't far behind. Only Grandpa and Uncle Charlie were in the kitchen when I entered.

"How's Mary?" I asked, and Grandpa told me that Lilli was up with her and she seemed to be doing fine.

I started pacing. Back and forth across the kitchen. I knew Uncle Nat had been with Lou when some of their babies were born, but that was one detail Mary and I had forgotten to talk about.

I wasn't sure I'd be good company in the birthing room. I was afraid I'd go and pass out or something right when Mary needed me the most. Oh, if only—if only there was some way that I could help her!

Lilli came down, her face a mite pale. She spoke as she walked right on by me to poke at the stove again.

"Mary wants you."

For a minute my feet wouldn't even move. I stood there, staring blankly after Lilli, licking dry lips and trying hard to swallow. And then I suddenly found my legs and propelled myself forward and up the steps.

Doc was bending over Mary, talking to her, calming her. I didn't want to get in his way so I went around to the other side. Mary, her face damp from her exertions, turned to look at me. She didn't say anything, just reached for my hand. I leaned over and kissed her on the forehead—right on the scar from her accident. Mary sort of buried her face against me for a moment, and then another contraction made her stiffen and pull away.

I looked at Doc. How could he stand this? She was—she was—

"She's doing fine. Just fine. You're doing just fine, Mary. Won't be too long and it'll all be over," Doc was murmuring, his voice more a drone than speech.

According to Doc, things progressed quickly. For me it seemed to take forever. But it did eventually come to an end. Like a wondrous miracle—one minute we were in the throes of birthing agony, and the next minute we were parents. *Parents*. I could hardly believe the fact even though I'd been waiting for it for months. But there he was—*our little son*—mine and Mary's. Red and wrinkled and wailing his head off.

I heard Mary chuckle and I wondered if she was totally aware or under the influence of some of Doc's ether. But she looked at me, her eyes big with wonder and then tears began to form and run down her cheeks. "A boy, Josh," she whispered. "A boy." And at that moment I knew that Mary had wanted with all her heart to present me with a son.

I leaned over to kiss her and smoothed the tangled hair back from her face. Oh, how I loved her. How I loved that new little bundle she had just presented to me. A son. Our very own son.

"William Joshua," I whispered, for that was the name we had already chosen.

"William Joshua," echoed Mary, and her eyes shone, the hours of pain totally forgotten. Just then Doc placed the still-squalling little bundle in Mary's arms.

"Isn't he beautiful?" Mary was crooning, and I had to admit that he was. *There's different kinds of beauty,* I thought with a smile as I looked into the little face all scrunched up with his efforts to cry.

Mary began to pat the baby and croon to him and the crying ceased. "I'll bet he's all tired out," she whispered. "It's hard work being born."

I hadn't thought of that. I had some idea now of how tough it was for Mary—for me—but for William Joshua? Maybe it was, I admitted.

I kissed Mary again—almost delirious in my happiness. Then I bent down to kiss the top of the head of our little child. He stirred a bit, and I pretended that he looked right at me and knew just who I was.

Mary pretended right along with me. "So, you are getting acquainted with your papa, William. You are one lucky boy. You have a wonderful papa. He'll take you fishin' an—"

Tears were on my cheeks. I hugged Mary and our son closer.

There was a tap at the door and I looked up, realizing then that Doc had quietly slipped from the room. It also dawned on me that there were some other anxious family members who were waiting down in the kitchen below.

Mary called, "Come in." And they were all there. Lilli and Grandpa and Uncle Charlie. The color was back in Lilli's cheeks and Grandpa was grinning like the world had just turned right side up and Uncle Charlie looked so relieved and proud at the same time that I wanted to chuckle.

They tiptoed in to peek at the small baby resting on Mary's arm.

"It's okay," said Mary. "He's awake."

Then they all started talking at once, saying what a fine baby he was and who he looked like and how alert he was and asked what we were going to name him and all that.

We had to slow them down and sort things out and finally were able to announce that his name was William Joshua. Grandpa looked across at me and nodded in understanding and agreement.

Doc returned and told us that Mary needed some rest. In spite of all the commotion, William Joshua had already fallen asleep. Lilli lifted him tenderly from Mary's arm and placed him in the nearby cradle. I went to look at him again, suddenly torn. I wanted to be near Mary, but I wanted to study my son. Doc settled it for me.

"Out with you, too, Josh," he informed me. "You can come back again when she's rested a bit."

I gave Mary one more kiss, took one last look at my son and reluctantly left the room. I didn't realize until I fell into one of the kitchen chairs how emotionally drained I was. I was glad for a cup of Lilli's coffee to sort of perk me up.

"How's the crop?" Grandpa asked, making conversation, and that brought the threshing sharply back to mind.

"I don't know," I admitted. "They were just starting to run some through."

I decided I'd best get back to the field and find out just what was happening.

CHAPTER 20

Tough Times

UNFORTUNATELY, THE CROP WAS even poorer than I expected. I should have known that it wouldn't be worth much, but I'd kept hoping that something might be in those near-empty heads. There wasn't much grain in the bins. It had me concerned, for a heavy farm payment was due at the bank. I knew it was going to be tough to cover it. We'd all have to tighten the belt. Considerably. But I hoped I wouldn't need to bother Mary with the worry of it.

Lilli stayed with us until Mary was back on her feet. Avery came whenever he could and spent the night. I knew he was anxious to get his wife home again.

William was an easy baby to have around. He scarcely cried at all, it seemed to me. But then I was in the fields or the barn a good deal of the time. Besides, William didn't have much need for fussin'. If Mary wasn't available, Grandpa or Uncle Charlie were. I figured as how they'd have that youngster spoiled long before he cut a tooth.

I put it off as long as I dared, and then one day I went out to make an honest assessment of the way things stood. I'd hated to face the truth, but the bank note was due the next Monday. I knew I had to figure out just how I was going to make the payment.

The picture wasn't a rosy one. There was barely enough seed grain to plant again come spring.

"If I can just make it through to another crop," I told myself, "then we'll be back on our feet again."

I reached a hand down into the bin and let the kernels of grain trickle through my fingers. Dwarfed and skimpy, they were nothing like the seed I had worked so hard to build up. But I was sure that with a couple years of good rains, I could be right back with good seed again.

I pulled a piece of paper from my hip pocket and a stub of a pencil from my shirt and started figuring. I had a little money laid aside, but it was nowhere near enough. There wasn't any grain to sell. I'd need every bit of it for seed come spring and to feed the cattle and hogs through the winter.

I jabbed at the paper with my pencil. Who was I trying to kid? There wasn't nearly enough grain to winter the stock. Some of the stock would have to go.

I had worked so hard to build up those bloodlines—some folks were saying I had the best breeding stock in the county. I sure didn't want to part with any of them.

But on the other hand, I reasoned, that would make them easier to sell—and at better prices.

I really got down to figuring then. After I had it all worked out on paper, I went back to the house.

Mary had dinner on the table. I crossed over to the cradle in the corner and looked down at my sleeping son. For once he wasn't being held by someone. He sure had changed already. His face was round and smooth and his nose and eyes were no longer red and swollen like they'd been when he was newborn. He had lost some of his dark hair too, but Mary didn't seem concerned about it. Babies did that, she said. Actually he was getting prettier and prettier—if boy babies don't mind being called "pretty." Lots of folks said he favored me, but every time I looked at him I saw glimpses of Mary.

"Been sleepin' like that most of the morning," boasted Mary. She had come to stand beside me. I slipped an arm around her waist and gave her a squeeze. The future didn't look nearly as bad with her beside me and our son to love and nourish.

"Your dinner's gettin' cold," Mary reminded me. I joined Grandpa and Uncle Charlie at the table, and we bowed our heads while I sincerely thanked God for His many blessings.

I could have discussed my plans over our noon meal, but I chose to wait until Mary and I were alone. William had awakened and insisted on being changed and fed immediately, and Mary cooed and smiled and went off to oblige. I went up to see them as soon as I had finished my bread pudding.

"He's been good, huh?" I asked, sitting beside Mary and lifting one of William's wee hands in mine. It looked rather lost there.

"Real good," said Mary, kissing his soft head.

We sat and admired William for a few minutes longer. He sure was growing fast.

"I'm going to be gone for most of the afternoon," I informed Mary.

She looked up, waiting.

"We'll need most of the crop for seed. I decided to sell off some of the stock so we don't need to worry none about winter feedin'."

"Couldn't we just buy us some more grain?" Mary asked innocently.

"I think it's better this way," I said without emotion. I didn't add that we didn't have money for more grain. Didn't even have enough money for the payment at the bank.

Mary nodded, quite willing that it would be my decision. She trusted me. That very fact made my stomach knot up.

"You going to ship?" she asked, knowing that market hogs and cattle were shipped from town by train.

"Think I'll give the local farmers a chance. They're always talkin' about my herds and wishin' they could add some of my stock to theirs."

Mary nodded again and I could see the pride in her eyes.

I kissed them both and went on down to saddle Chester.

I rode all afternoon—from farm to farm, and the story was always the same. No one had feed. No one had money. Over and over I heard the same words.

"Boy, I'd like to, Josh. Been wantin' to get some of yer stock fer a long time. But right now ain't a good time. Crop too poor. No feed. No money. Maybe next year after we git 'nother crop in the bins."

But next year wouldn't help my dilemma. I needed cash *now*.

By the end of the day I was about spent. It wasn't just that the ride had been tiring. It was the whole emotional drain of the process. And I'd been unsuccessful. I would need to resort to shipping the stock, and I knew the price I got for slaughter animals would not be nearly as good as that paid for breeding stock.

I hated to go home and face Mary. I was afraid she would read in my eyes the fear I felt inside.

I tried to shake off my foreboding. We'd make it. It would just be tough for a while and then the crops would get us on our feet again. All we had to do was make that bank payment and ease our way through the year until the crop was up again. We could make it. It would be good for us to have to cut back a bit. Make us even more appreciative of the good harvest—the bountiful times.

Before I went into the house I sat down on a milk stool and pulled out my paper and pencil again. It would take more critters than I had first counted on to make the payment. It was really going to cut into the herd to meet that bank commitment. And I'd have to go see the banker the first thing in the morning and ask for a few days' extension. There was no way I could get my payment in the mail in time for the original deadline. I hoisted myself off the stool and tucked away my figurings.

Mary gave me a smile when I entered the kitchen, but she didn't ask about my day. I was glad. I didn't have an answer quite ready yet.

It wasn't until we were retiring that night that the subject was discussed. Mary waited until William had been changed and fed and tucked in for the night. After we had finished our regular devotions together, I stretched out full length beneath the fresh-smelling sheets and was about to shut my eyes, hoping for early sleep and maybe postponement of a difficult discussion. But Mary slipped her hand into mine.

"How'd it go, Josh?" she asked me.

I hesitated for just a moment and then answered honestly, "Not good."

She was silent, giving me a chance to go on.

"Oh, everywhere I went folks were anxious enough to buy. They just don't have any feed either. I should've thought of that. Whole country was dry this year."

"Any way to get the stock to where folks *do* have feed?" asked Mary, and I wondered why I hadn't thought of that. I lay there thinking about it now—but came up empty.

"I wouldn't know how," I admitted. "From the reports in the paper and on the radio, the dryness has covered a large area. I have no idea where folks might have more feed than critters." I sighed deeply and Mary's hand tightened on mine. "Besides," I went on, "I would have no way of making contacts or of getting the animals beyond the county."

"What are you going to do?" asked Mary.

"Ship. Market them. There's another market day on Thursday. I'll get 'em in for that."

I had to round up a crew of neighbor boys to help me drive my stock to town. It seemed that every farmer in the whole area was like-minded. When I arrived with my cattle, the holding pens were already filled to near bursting. I knew without thinking on it that I needed to knock a few more dollars off the price I would get for the animals. It always happened that way when the market was flooded. I wished I'd brought along a few more yearlings.

The bank manager was decent enough. He admitted that it had been a tough year—that all the area farmers were having a hard time. He said the same thing that I had been saying to myself—over and over. Things would all straighten out next year when the crop was taken in.

There was nothing for me to do then but to wait for that stock payment to arrive in the mail. I thought of it constantly. Prayed that it would be enough. But it wasn't. Not quite. I took it to the banker and promised to sell a couple more cattle. He nodded solemnly and applied to the loan what I had brought.

Mary knew I was troubled. She left me alone for several days, and then I guess she decided we needed to talk about it.

"How bad is it, Josh?" she asked and I knew that she wanted, and deserved, an honest answer.

"Pretty bad," I admitted. "But it'll be all right. I made the loan payment. I was sorry to sell as much stock as it turned out I needed to, that's all. It was good stock. Too good for slaughtering. It should have been used to help other farmers build their herds. But it couldn't be helped. Everybody's having a tough time. No feed. Prices down. It just couldn't be helped. We get these cycles from time to time—and then things bounce back. We'll be all right with another crop."

"Anything I can do?"

I could have said, "Economize. Watch each dollar. Skimp all you can." But I didn't need to say those things. I knew Mary would do that without me asking.

"We'll make it," I said instead.

We lay in silence, each with our own thoughts.

"We have the egg money," Mary offered.

I drew her up against my side. I knew she'd stretch that egg money for all it was worth.

CHAPTER 21

Planting Again

WINTER DRAGGED BY ON reluctant feet. I guess I was just too anxious for spring to come so that I could get to the planting again. I was weary of trying to make each dollar stretch and of seeing Mary skimp and save. She never complained though. Nor did anyone else in the household.

The little snow that did fall was soon blown into small, dirty piles mixed with top soil from the parched fields. I'm sure if we'd had seven feet of snow that winter, none of the neighborhood farmers would have complained.

Our William gained weight steadily and became more interesting—more of a "real person"—with each day. He was our bit of sunshine over a bleak winter, and the hours of playing with him and hearing his squeals and giggles more than brightened our lives.

The whole household doted on him, but thankfully he didn't seem to get spoiled. He contentedly lay in his cradle and talked to himself as he tried to catch his chubby toes or the items that Mary dangled over his head.

At last the days began to warm into some kind of spring. I finally decided I could start work on the land. I didn't need to wait for the snow to melt—there was none. I didn't need to wait for the fields to dry either. The stubble was dry as tinder. I didn't use the tractor. There was simply no money for fuel, so I hitched up the farm horses and began to farm the way the land had been farmed for many years before me.

I'd forgotten how much slower going it was with horses. Often my eyes would wander to the shed where the tractor sat silent. The row of shiny, unused farm machinery I had bought over the past few years to pull behind it seemed to mournfully becken me. I longed to return it all to use. There was no use moaning. This spring it was not meant to be. As I planted I told myself that things would be better next spring.

I came in from the field each day dusty, tired and sometimes a bit out of sorts. The ground I turned with the plow was powdery or chunky hard; and as my eyes watched the clouds, I saw no sign of spring rains.

Mary tried to keep everyone's spirits up with talk of how well the chickens were laying and how perfect the new calves were and what a good litter the last sow had given us. I knew I should be thankful. I really was thankful, but in the back of my mind was the nagging doubt that all those things might not be enough.

I'd hoped for a rain before I actually did the spring planting, but when all of the land had been tilled and still dry as a bone, I decided to plant anyway. If I got the grain in the ground and the rains quickly followed, I'd be even further ahead. Yes, I decided, that was a good plan.

So I planted the seed—every last kernel I had. Placed it right there in the dry ground with the faith that every farmer must have each spring—the faith that at the proper time, within the structure that God has ordained for seed time and harvest, the rain would come, the seed would germinate and a harvest would result.

The grain lay for a week before a cloud even appeared in the sky. It didn't develop into much, but we did get a light sprinkle. I knew it had scarcely dampened the ground. Still, it brought hope. The whole town was buzzing with talk of it when I drove in to pick up groceries and the mail. Everyone was hopeful that there would be more clouds coming with spring rains in the normal fashion, and I came home in much better spirits. I guess all the jovial bantering and lighter chatter had helped.

Mary smiled as I placed the few staples on her kitchen table.

"Did we get a letter?" she asked hopefully. I was usually excited when we received one of our rather rare letters. I shook my head but grinned at Mary in my new-found cheer.

Grandpa wandered over to the table and listlessly turned over the two small sales pamphlets. He missed his daily paper—as we all did. The paper was just one of the things we needed to forego during our belt-tightening time.

"Farmers are pretty excited about the shower," I reported to Mary but including Grandpa and Uncle Charlie also.

"Say that it's most certain to stir up some more storms," I went on.

Grandpa nodded. "Gotta be rain up there somewhere," he agreed.

Uncle Charlie used his two canes to lift himself from his chair by the window and join the rest of us at the table.

"They reportin' how much they got?"

This was common talk when farmer met farmer. "Had three quarters of an inch over our way, but Fred says thet he got a full inch." Or, "That heavy shower dumped two an' a half inches at my place." Always the rains were measured, the amount that fell of utmost importance.

I shook my head. "No one seemed to get more'n we did—didn't measure much. But it's a good sign."

Grandpa and Uncle Charlie both nodded, relief in their eyes. Mary said nothing, but she went to the cupboard and got out the coffee. She put the pot on to brew, and the aroma of it was soon wafting out deliciously around us.

We all settled in around the table with pleased looks on our faces. It was the first time in months that we'd shared afternoon coffee. There hadn't even been before-bed coffee for Grandpa and Uncle Charlie anymore. It was another of the things we had learned to do without. Coffee—weak coffee—was reserved for breakfast, and each of us was allowed only one cup a day. Mary never touched it. She said that her nursing baby was better off without it, though Doc had said a cup of coffee wouldn't hurt young William. I figured Mary was just going without to save more for the rest of us.

It wasn't hard for me to go without—and I often did. Said I didn't feel like a cup, or it wouldn't sit quite right on my stomach, or something, and shared the cup with Grandpa and Uncle Charlie. Not a sacrifice for me. I could drink it or leave it. But Grandpa and Uncle Charlie were another matter. Especially that before-bed cup. They had done it all their lives as far back as I could remember.

So the coffee aroma that drifted to us was a celebration

of sorts. And we all knew it. I guess that made it even more special.

Mary went even further. She sliced some bread and spread some of her carefully hoarded strawberry jam over it—thinly, I might point out. She set this on the table to go with the coffee.

Boy, what a feast! More than the coffee and jam was the promise. We'd had one rain—only a shower, really—but a rain. It meant that we'd probably be getting more, that things would soon be back to normal again. And what a relief that would be to us all.

But it didn't happen that way. A few more clouds rolled up, and we all hoped and prayed that they would bring us moisture. But the wind blew them right on by without so much as a sprinkle. Even the pasture land was beginning to look like barren ground. I knew I had too many cows feeding on it and that I should sell off a few more. But I just kept putting it off and putting it off, hoping and praying that rain would soon have things green again.

At last I remembered the good advice I'd received from Mr. Thomas, the farmer who years before had kindly showed me the proper way to farm. "A few good, healthy cattle are better than a bunch of skinny, sickly ones," he'd said, and I finally gave in and made arrangements to get half a dozen of them to town.

I didn't spend the money I got for them but tucked it away. Besides, it wasn't all that much anyway and wouldn't have made much difference in how we were living. The price of cattle had dropped something awful.

The hot, thirsty summer was a repeat of the previous one. As I walked about the farm trying to keep the barns and fences in order, my feet kicked up little puffs of dirt and sent them sifting up to stick to my overalls or drift away on the wind that was constantly blowing.

I'd never seen so much wind. The continual howling nearly got Mary down. She complained about few things—but the wind was one of them. I saw her unconsciously shudder when a gust rattled the windows or whipped grit against the panes.

All summer long she fought to save her garden. With our finances as they were, it was even more important that she have produce to can or store in the nearby root cellar. Day by day she carried water by the pail and dumped it on her plants, coaxing them, imploring them to bring her fruit.

Grandpa helped all he could, huffing and puffing under the heat of the sun and against the strength of the wind. Uncle Charlie was past the stage of being able to carry buckets, so he stationed himself beside William's cradle and watched over the sleeping baby in Mary's absence.

The garden did produce—but all of us knew that it wouldn't really be enough to see us through another winter with any kind of ease.

Toward the end of summer another calamity struck. The well that had served us faithfully for as many years as the farm had stood went dry. Grandpa himself had dug it and it had never failed before. I guess we'd always assumed that our water supply was unlimited. But now, no matter how hard I pumped, there was only a small trickle, and then we had to wait a few hours until we could produce a trickle again.

It was heartbreaking, especially for Mary. There was no way she could help her plants now. She left them to the elements, canning what she could as soon as it was ready.

I was thankful for the crick for the sake of the stock, but even the crick was lower than I'd ever seen it before.

There wasn't much to harvest that fall, but we went through the motions. I did manage to salvage a bit of grain that I hoarded away carefully for next spring's seed.

Surely next year would be different. We'd had dry spells before, but they'd never lasted for more than a year or two. We all set our jaws and readied ourselves for another slim winter.

William celebrated his first birthday. Or rather, we adults celebrated for him. He did seem to enjoy the occasion. We had a whole houseful over, almost like old times again. Nat and Lou and their family came along with Avery and Lilli. The house was alive and full of laughter and cheerful chatter, and William laughed and clapped and chattered right along with us.

No fuss was made, but each family brought simple food items with them. Lou had a big pot of rabbit stew and some pickled beets. Lilli brought deviled eggs and a crock of kraut. With the roast chicken Mary prepared in our kitchen, we had ourselves quite a feast. There was even a cake for the birthday boy—and some weak tea for the adults.

Sarah appointed herself William's guardian. She hardly let the rest get a chance to hold and cuddle him. But over her protests he did make the rounds. He was walking now, faltering baby steps that made everyone squeal with delight and William beam over his own brilliance. He seemed to know just how smart he was and spent his time toddling back and forth between eager, outstretched hands.

It was a great day for all of us, but when it was over and a thoroughly exhausted William had been tucked into bed, a sense of dejection seemed to settle over the house. It was as though we had been released from our prison for one short afternoon and had then been rounded up and locked up again. The day had been a reminder of how things had been, and maybe each of us secretly feared it would never really be that way again.

We didn't speak of it, but we all knew it was there—a fear hanging right over us, seeming about to consume us, to hold us under until we ran out of air or to squeeze us into a corner until we stopped our struggling.

I didn't like the feeling. I wanted to break loose and breathe freely again. I wanted my wife to sew new dresses and cook from a well-stocked cupboard. I wanted my son to have those first little shoes for his growing feet, toy trucks and balls to play with. I wanted Grandpa and Uncle Charlie to be able to sit around the kitchen table and sip slowly from big cups of strong coffee.

For the first time in my adult life, I wanted to sit down and weep in frustration. And then I looked across the table to where Mary sat mending work socks. They had more darning than original wool, and I saw the frustration in her eyes. By the stubborn set to her chin I knew she was feeling the same way I was. It put some starch in my backbone.

"Why don't you leave that for tonight?" I suggested to her. "It's been a busy day."

I went to the stove and shook the coffeepot. There was just a tiny bit remaining. I poured in more water from the teakettle that sang near the back of the stove and set the pot on to boil.

"Bit left there yet," I said to Grandpa. "Why don't you and Uncle Charlie finish it up?"

Grandpa nodded without much enthusiasm. He was feeling it too.

I took the sock from Mary's hands, laid it aside and then led her up the stairs to our room.

We didn't talk much as we prepared for bed. As soon as we were both ready, I lifted our family Bible down from the shelf.

We always read together before retiring. There was nothing new about that. What was different was the way I was feeling deep down inside.

"Would you read tonight?" I asked Mary.

She took the Bible from me and turned to the book of Psalms. Given a choice, Mary always turned to the Psalms. She began with a praise chapter—one that was meant to lift my spirits and bring me comfort. It should have done that for me. I had much to praise God for. But tonight—tonight the praise seemed all locked up within me. Mary hadn't read far before I was weeping.

I would never be able to explain why. Maybe I had just been carrying the hurts and the worries for too long, I don't know. Maybe I'd been trying to be too brave to protect the rest of my family. Anyway, it all poured out in rasping sobs that shook my whole body. Mary joined me and we held each other and cried together.

After the tempest had passed and we were in control again, we lay for hours and talked. Just talked, until long into the night. I don't know that we solved anything, but we lifted a big burden from each other. We shared our feelings and our fears. We joined, strength with strength, to weather whatever lay before us.

"We'll make it, Josh," Mary dared to promise.

"I still have the loan payment to make," I confided. "I only have a small portion of it saved, and I've no idea how I'll get the rest."

"We have more livestock."

"I hate to sell—"

"But we'll build the herd again. After the rains come—"

Always. Always that was our answer. Things would be better. We'd be back on our feet—after the spring rains came.

Chapter 22

Hope Upon Hope

I NEVER WEPT OVER our situation again. Not that I viewed tears as weakness. Maybe I hurt so deeply that I knew tears would not ease the pain. Or maybe I came to a higher level of faith. For whatever reason, I never came near to tears again.

I sold off more of the livestock. There really wasn't much choice, but it pained me to see the herd I'd worked so hard to build less than half its former size. With the sale of the stock, plus what I'd managed to tuck aside and a bit of Mary's hard-won egg and cream money, we somehow managed to make another loan payment.

But that meant there was little money to tide us over the winter months. I took my rifle and hunted grouse and rabbit and managed to add a bit to the stew pot. Mary talked of butchering a few chickens, but she hesitated. We'd already used all the old hens and all but two of the roosters.

"It's sort of like killing the goose that laid the golden egg,"

Mary commented to me. "We need those eggs—both for ourselves and to sell in town."

I knew Mary was right, so we held off dipping into the flock further.

Then I thought about the piece of treed crick bottom on the Turley land, and I decided there might be a bit of money in cord wood. Mary clutched at the idea right away, her eyes shining.

"What a wonderful idea, Josh!" she exclaimed. "But I do hope the work won't be too hard on you."

"It's not the work that worries me," I admitted. "We'll need to find a buyer before it means any money."

"Oh, I'm sure we'll find somebody," she enthused. "Everyone needs firewood—even in hard times."

It turned out that we were able to sell it. All I could cut, the buyer at the lumberyard said. It seemed that he had some kind of connection with city folk and shipped the wood out by rail car.

But the earnings were a mere pittance. Took me two or three days of back-breaking labor to make enough to buy flour and sugar. Rumors were that the man from the lumberyard made himself a pretty good profit just to act as go-between. It bothered me some, but I felt I had little to say in the matter. I kept at it. At least it might see us through another winter.

I used Barney and Bess for the skidding, alternating them day by day. I didn't have the feed or the chop I normally would have been feeding my horses, so I liked to rest them as much as I could. Chester was a bit too light for the hard work or he would have done his share, too.

Somehow we managed. It was tough, but we all were able to keep body and soul together. I was thankful for that much.

The second winter of scanty snow came to an end. When the patches of dirty drifts melted, I was back on the land again.

It didn't take as long as usual to do the spring work. I didn't have enough seed grain to plant all of the fields. There was no use working up those that couldn't be planted. The soil would just erode even more.

Mary planted her garden too. She had carefully kept every possible seed so she wouldn't need to buy. She even exchanged some with neighborhood women. All together, she managed to get a reasonable garden in the ground. She knew better than to even start drawing water from the well. There simply wasn't enough there. She saved every bit of dishwater and wash water that was used, though, and carefully doled it out to her plants.

I had never seen anything like the dust storms that came that year. They rolled up from the west, raising hopes that maybe a rain cloud was on the way, and then blew in with nothing but flying dirt and empty promises. Dust lay over everything. Whole fields seemed to be airborne, swirling madly about us. Mary came to hate the dust even worse than the wind.

Along with the dust came the grasshoppers. There wasn't much for them to eat, but they seemed to flourish anyway. I knew even without walking through the fields that there would be *no* crop this year. I went back to cutting cord wood.

Near the end of August Uncle Charlie took sick. It was a Sunday morning, and Mary had our breakfast on the table and William all ready to go to church. Uncle Charlie still hadn't made his appearance. It wasn't like him. He lingered in bed now and then, having spent a restless night, but never on a Sunday morning.

We sat down to the table, our eyes on the stairway, thinking surely he'd be showing up at any minute.

Mary turned to me. "Do you think you should check, Josh?" she asked.

William pounded his spoon impatiently on the table and called in his babyish lisp, "Eat time. Eat time, Unc'a Shar-ie."

Grandpa forgot his worry long enough to have a good chuckle at William. Mary stopped the boy from banging his spoon, and I looked toward the stairs again.

I went on up then, and there was Uncle Charlie on the floor beside his bed. He must have been trying to get out of bed when he took a fall.

It scared me, I'll tell you. It frightened all of us. We abandoned our plans for church. Grandpa and I lifted Uncle Charlie back onto his bed, and I saddled Chester and headed out for Doc.

By the time we got back, Uncle Charlie was conscious and rational. He still wanted to go to church, but Doc said he had a pretty nasty bump on the head and was to stay in bed for a few days. Besides, it was already too late for church anyway.

After Doc had done all he could to make Uncle Charlie comfortable and left a bit of medicine for him, Doc and I walked down to the kitchen. Mary had poured a cup of morning coffee and set it at the table for him. She'd fed William, but the rest of us still had not had our breakfast. The familiar morning oatmeal had not improved with age, but we ate it anyway. It did fill the void.

Doc sat down for a neighborly visit. He told Mary of new babies in the community—even shared the secret of a few on the way, and told of people in town moving in and those who were moving out. He even shared bits and pieces of world news—things that we would have been getting out of the newspaper had we still been receiving one.

And then he turned his attention to William.

"Your boy sure looks healthy," he said to Mary, and Mary beamed.

"Come here, fella," Doc called to the toddler, and William trotted over to be lifted up on Doc's knee.

"You ever see one of these?" Doc asked and dangled his stethoscope before William. I don't suppose there was a kid in our whole area who hadn't played with Doc's stethoscope at one time or another. And it had fascinated every one of us, too. William was no exception. He turned it around and around in his hand, then tried to stick the smooth, round end into his ear.

We all laughed.

"So you're going to be a doctor someday," commented Doc. "But you've got it backward. This is what goes in your ears. Here, hold still."

He helped the little fella with the instrument, and William's eyes grew wide with wonder. I had a pretty good idea that he was hearing absolutely nothing, but the feeling of something holding his head from each side must have intrigued him. He sat perfectly still until Doc removed the ear pieces.

"Well, I'd best be running," Doc said at last. "Someone might be needing me."

He lifted William to the floor and reached for his hat. "Yes, sir," he said, his eyes still on William. "You're a nice, big boy for two years old. Almost two years old," he corrected himself. "Your mama has taken real good care of you."

I walked with Doc to get his team. It was an awkward moment for me. I hardly knew where or how to begin.

"Doc," I finally blurted, "in the past we've always paid you cash for your visits, but I'm afraid—"

Doc stopped me before I could even go on. "I know how

things are right now, Josh," he returned confidentially. "We'll just put this here little visit on your account."

"But I don't have an account," I reminded him.

"You do now," said Doc, "and don't you go worrying none about it either. You can take care of it just as soon as you get another crop."

Doc came three more times to visit Uncle Charlie. On his last visit Mary had a little chat with him too. It seemed her suspicions were correct. She was expecting our second child.

I should have been happy—and I was. But this time I was worried too. How would we ever feed and clothe another child? William was already doing without things he should have had—and he was better off than most of the children in our area. Lou passed on to him many of the things Jonathan and Timothy had worn.

But in spite of morning sickness again, Mary was happy. It fell to Grandpa to entertain young William until Mary was able to be on her feet. I was still busy with cutting wood and unable to give much assistance in the house.

Uncle Charlie got steadily better, to our great relief. By the time William celebrated his second birthday, Uncle Charlie was again able to join us at the table. By then Mary was feeling much better, too.

There wasn't any crop to harvest, so I just kept right on working in the woodlot. Now and then the lumberyard owner would pop by and have the wood loaded onto a truck and hauled to the railway yards. He'd pay me each time he made a pickup, and I tried hard to put some of it aside. But there wasn't much of it in the drawer when I went to count up the money. I'd needed to spend most of it for necessities throughout the summer and fall. I would have to sell stock again. Even with the sale, I wondered if it would be enough to meet the payment. My heart sank at the thought.

I was heading for my room to do some more figuring when Grandpa's voice stopped me.

I turned to look at him. He and Uncle Charlie were at the kitchen table. There was no coffee to drink, but maybe it was hard to break an old habit. Anyway, they still pulled up their chairs each evening and sat there—chatting, even playing an occasional game of checkers. But often they just sat, waiting for the time to go to bed.

Mary had already gone up to tuck William in for the night, and I knew it wouldn't be long until she would be waiting for our devotional time together.

"Got a minute?"

I nodded.

"Charlie and I think it's time we talk."

I didn't have any idea what was coming but I felt my stomach began to tighten.

"You got another payment to make," Grandpa said as I pulled out a chair and lowered myself onto it. It was a statement—not a question.

I nodded again.

There was silence for a minute. Uncle Charlie sucked in air, much as he used to suck in coffee.

"You got it figured?" went on Grandpa.

I lowered my head for a moment and then brought it up to face the two men. "No-o," I admitted. "No—not yet."

"In thet case," said Grandpa, shoving a lidded tin toward me, "we want ya to have this."

I looked from Grandpa to Uncle Charlie.

"If we'd 'a knowed what straights you was in, we'd 'a given it long ago. Feel bad we've been lettin' ya sweat it out alone," said Uncle Charlie, an unusually long speech for him.

"It's the Turley farm," I admitted. "It probably was a mistake to take on more land, especially with the drought."

"I figured it a smart move," Grandpa hurried to say. "One ya couldn't pass up, really. Just a shame thet we been prayin' fer rain ever since. But thet'll change. Just need time, thet's all. Just time."

I appreciated Grandpa's vote of confidence and Uncle Charlie's nod of agreement. Then Grandpa pushed the can farther toward me and this time I reached out for it.

I pulled it to me and pried off the lid.

I stared in disbelief. It was full of bills.

"It ain't much," Grandpa was saying, "but it might help some."

I knew then what I was looking at. It was the total life's savings of Grandpa and Uncle Charlie. I pushed the can back toward them, fighting hard to swallow.

"I can't—I can't take that," I finally was able to say.

"What'll ya do then?" asked Grandpa without hesitation.

"I—I—" I swallowed. "I still have some stock. I can sell—"

"We been thinkin' on thet," said Grandpa. "It don't seem like a good move. I mean—ya sell it all off an' then where are ya? Soon as the rains start up agin, ya got no herd to build on."

I knew he was right. I'd thought that all through myself and come to the same conclusion.

"We don't know when the rains—" I began, but Grandpa cut in.

"They'll come," he said simply. "Always do."

But when, I wanted to cry out. *When? After it's too late—after we've lost everything?*

I didn't say it. Instead, I looked first at Grandpa and then at Uncle Charlie.

"It might not be enough," Grandpa was saying. "We don't know how big those payments be. But take it. Make it do fer ya what ya can."

"But you've worked all your life to save this money," I persisted. "I can't just take it and—"

Uncle Charlie waved an arthritic hand as though to brush aside all my arguments. "Josh," he said, "you've been boardin' an' beddin' us fer several years now. Ain't either of us worth a lick a salt. But ya ain't hinted at thet. Neither has Mary. Now, iffen the farm goes—then what, Josh? This is our home too, an' I reckon as how we'd be hard put adjustin' to 'nother one."

" 'Zactly," agreed Grandpa.

"But—" I tried again.

"No 'buts,' Josh. Just take it on in an' make thet there payment, iffen it'll do thet, an' get thet monkey off all our backs."

I had no further arguments. I thanked the two men before me as sincerely as I could and tucked the tin under my arm. I had no idea how much money was in the can. It wouldn't be much, I knew. Grandpa and Uncle Charlie had never had the opportunity to stash away large sums. But maybe—just maybe it would be enough to keep us afloat. Maybe—just maybe—it would help us make it to another spring.

CHAPTER 23

Sustained Effort

THERE WAS ENOUGH IN the tin can to make the loan payment—with some left over to help us through the winter. I went to town the next morning with the money tied securely in my coat pocket.

I was getting to hate trips to town and avoided them whenever possible. It seemed whenever I went there was news of another foreclosure and another area farmer forced off his land.

It wasn't as hard for those who had been there for years and were well established. Some had no payments due at the bank and could manage to sort of slide by even though money was tight. But for those who had just invested in land or stock or new machinery, the matter was quite different. It was almost impossible to stay afloat, given the economics of the times along with the drought.

It saddened me. I guess it also frightened me. The thought kept nagging at me that my turn might be next.

I didn't know what I'd ever do if I lost the farm. It wasn't just the fact that I loved it—had always loved it. I figured I had about as much of that farm soil running through my veins as I had red blood. I couldn't imagine myself anywhere but on that farm.

Grandpa had settled the farm. He and Uncle Charlie had sweated and toiled and built it to what it had become. It belonged to us. To all of us. It belonged to my son some time down the road.

Farming was all I knew. I was not trained for anything else. I had no other home, no other possession, no other profession. If I lost the farm I would lose far more than a piece of property. I would lose my livelihood, my heritage, my family home, my very sense of personhood. I wouldn't fit any other place. I knew that without going through the experience.

And knowing all of that, and knowing also that Grandpa and Uncle Charlie shared my feelings, I took the gift of money they had given me and tried to buy the family a little more time. And I prayed that they were right. That the rains were soon due back again.

I felt better after I had made the payment. I didn't miss the surprised look on the banker's face when I drew out the small roll of bills, but he asked no questions and I volunteered no information. I was handed my receipt of payment and left the building.

I stopped long enough to buy a few groceries, among the parcels a pound of coffee for Grandpa and Uncle Charlie and some cheese for Mary. She had made several remarks over the last few days about how good cheese would taste. Then I bought a sack of grain to feed her chickens. It would do us all well if we could keep the hens laying.

I was about to head for home when I remembered to pick up the mail. There rarely was anything of importance, but I checked it out anyway. Later I wished I hadn't even gone to the post office.

Mr. Hiram Smith was ahead of me at the wicket. "Howdy, Josh," he hailed me and I returned his greeting.

"Another rough summer," he commented sociably and I agreed that it was.

"Hear more farmers are having a hard time."

I nodded to that too.

"Did you have any crop at all?" he asked.

"Not much," I admitted. "I turned the cows on it. Wasn't worth the time of trying to harvest it."

It was his turn to nod. "Too bad," he pondered. "Sure too bad. Farms're up for sale all over the place." He didn't even wait for a response from me. "Trouble is," he went on, "no buyers. Why, ya can't even give one away. Nobody's got money to buy. That's how it is. Too bad."

It was all the truth—but it was all old news by now. I was about to ask for my mail and move on.

"Ya hear 'bout Avery?" asked Mr. Smith.

I hadn't, and I stopped mid-stride. I wasn't sure I wanted to hear about Avery if it was going to be bad news—and from Mr. Smith's expression, it looked as if it would be. But Avery was my brother-in-law. If there was something wrong, I had to know.

"Lost his farm," said Mr. Smith, rather callously to my thinking. "Just gettin' started, too. An' him newly married an' all. Too bad." He shook his head one more time and moved toward the door, shuffling through advertising flyers as he did so.

I went all sick inside.

It was Mary that I thought of first. I knew how deeply the news would trouble her. *Poor Mary. And poor Lilli—and her expecting their first child too,* I mourned.

Now the postmaster took up the tale of woe. "Sure too bad. Sure too bad," he repeated as he shook his head much as Mr. Smith had done. "Me, I can't even keep up with the comin' an' goin' anymore. Move in—move out. Jest like that. One after the other—"

"Where—where did Avery—?"

"Oh, he didn't move. Least not away from the area. He jest moved on home again with his folks. Same mailbox as always." The most important thing to the postmaster seemed to be keeping his mailboxes straight. I started to move away.

"Don'tcha want your mail?" he called after me, and I turned back. There was one letter addressed to Mrs. Joshua Jones and a few advertising pieces. I threw the flyers in the wastebasket as I walked past it, and stuck the letter for Mary in my pocket.

I couldn't get Avery and Lilli out of my mind as I headed the team for home. Most of all I dreaded telling the news to Mary. But I knew she had to be told.

I broke it to her as gently as I could and held her while she wept. Then we bundled up, left William in Grandpa and Uncle Charlie's care, and drove over to Avery's folks.

Just as I had been told in town, we heard directly from Avery that he had lost his farm. He was pretty down about it, but Lilli was keeping her chin up.

"We'll try again—later," she said confidently, "when the crops are growing again and the rains are back."

In the meantime she was sharing a house with five other people and her child would soon be number six.

"How are you?" Mary whispered to her.

"Fine. Fine," she insisted. "Just anxious to get it all over with. Only three more weeks now. That's not so long."

But the house was already crowded. Avery and Lilli had a very small bedroom off the kitchen. I couldn't help but wonder where they would squeeze in a small crib.

Times were tough. Really tough. But at least they had a roof over their heads.

In all the turmoil I had forgotten to give Mary her letter. I found it that night as I undressed for bed.

"Oh, I'm sorry," I apologized. "I forgot to give you this. I picked it up at the post office today."

I didn't add that I was more than a mite curious about the letter.

Mary tore the envelope open quickly and withdrew one formal looking page. She scanned it, then went back to read it more slowly. She looked pleased with the contents. I was relieved. I was afraid it might be more bad news.

"It's from the school-board chairman," she told me. "I wrote inquiring about boarding the teacher."

I was surprised. Mary had said nothing about it.

"He's happy to have him stay here," Mary continued. "The place where he's been boarding hasn't worked out well."

I knew that the present schoolteacher was a middle-aged, single man. He had been the butt of many community jokes, a rather strange, eccentric fellow.

I looked at Mary again.

"Are you sure you want to take him on?" I asked her.

"Can't you see?" said Mary. "This is a direct answer to my prayers. I asked God what I might do to ease our situation, and He brought this to my mind. So I wrote the letter and left it with God—and He has worked it out so that Mr. Butler is willing to stay here."

"But—" I began, but Mary wasn't finished.

"The money will help buy groceries for all of us, and I might even be able to help with the loan payment."

"But the work," I protested. "You have more than enough now, and with the new baby—"

Mary waved that argument aside too. "Grandpa helps in the kitchen and Uncle Charlie keeps William entertained. Mr. Butler will be gone most of the day and will be leavin' every weekend. Won't be much extra work at all."

She had it all figured. I couldn't help but chuckle.

"You're really somethin'," I said to Mary, gathering her into my arms. She just smiled and let the letter flutter to the floor.

Much to my dismay, Mr. Butler arrived with a spirited horse and a buggy. There had been no warning that I would be expected to stable a horse and provide feed. I couldn't even feed my own horses properly.

But even before I could raise the question Mr. Butler explained, "I've arranged for Lady Jane to be housed"—"housed," he said—"at the school barn. Todd Smith will be her groom."

I nodded, relieved. *A "groom," no less.*

"I needed the buggy to bring my things," he went on.

His "things" consisted of several trunks and suitcases and a couple of carpet bags. I wondered how he would fit it all in the small bedroom off the kitchen and still leave himself walking room. I never did find out, for I never entered the room after

Mr. Butler took possession, and he always kept his door tightly closed.

Even Mary didn't go in that room. Mr. Butler preferred to do his own "keeping." Once a week Mary laid out fresh linens and towels and Mr. Butler replaced them with the soiled ones. It was a good arrangement for Mary.

He was a strange-looking little man, all right. A large nose dominated his small face, and his chin was almost nonexistent. Eyes, dark and piercing, hid behind thick, heavy-rimmed glasses. He was bald. At least I'm pretty sure he was, but he had this trick of combing his hair from deep down on the side and bringing it across the top to join the other side so you didn't really see the baldness. When he stepped out into the wind, he was very careful to pull his hat down securely until it almost included his ears. I couldn't help but wonder if he had nightmares about it suddenly blowing off, his hair flying straight up in the air, waving to all those who watched as his bald spot was exposed to the world.

He didn't have much to say to us grown-ups, but he took to William right away. With his love for children, I guess he made a good school teacher. Anyway, the time he spent in the kitchen with the rest of the family was whiled away with William and picture books. He would pull a chair near the warmth of the kitchen stove, lift William on his knee and spread out a book before them. They spent hours together, his quiet voice explaining to William the wonders of the Wall of China, the mysteries of the planet Mars, the secrets of the ancient Egyptians or the flight patterns of tiny hummingbirds. I'd look across at Mary and suppress a chuckle, or at Grandpa or Uncle Charlie with a wink. William might be a sharp little fella, but what could a child of two possibly understand of all that?

Still, William went right back for more—every time he had the opportunity. And he sat there on that teacher's knee and drank in every word, his eyes wide with wonder, his chubby finger pointing at the pictures, his baby voice trying to repeat some of the difficult words.

When Mary would announce that it was William's bedtime, the teacher always looked rather disappointed, but he lifted William carefully down, closed his book and retired to his room.

We made it through another winter and I began to scan the skies looking for rain clouds. Though clouds did form from time to time, they just didn't seem to have much moisture in them. But I scraped together enough money to buy a bit of seed grain and planted a couple of my fields.

The birth of William had interrupted the harvest. Now the arrival of our second child brought me in from the planting to ride off for Doc.

Everything went fine, and before I could scarcely draw a breath, our second son joined the family. As soon as I had breathed a prayer of thankfulness that Mary and the baby were both fine, the reality of another doctor's bill took some of the pleasure from the occasion.

"I'll just add it to your account, Josh," Doc said quietly as I went with him later to get his buggy. We were getting ourselves quite a sizable account with Doc.

Our new boy was another beautiful baby. Plump and healthy with lusty lungs. William studied him in awe. Not until the new baby finally closed his eyes and his loud little mouth and went to sleep could we get William close enough to actually reach out a hand and touch him on the cheek. From then on he seemed quite pleased with his baby brother.

We named him Daniel Charles after Grandpa and Uncle Charlie, and the two men beamed as we announced the name.

We found a neighbor girl to take over the kitchen duties until Mary was able to be up and about, and somehow we managed. Baby Daniel settled into the family unit just fine, and I finished my bit of planting and went back to the woodlot again.

More of my fields drifted away as spring gave way to summer. I could only hope that some of the soil from many miles away might stop at my land. If the wind didn't work out some kind of exchange, I feared there would soon be no more topsoil to farm.

Poor Mary struggled with her garden. It was hard, discouraging work. Not much grew and the grasshoppers relished the bit that was there.

School ended and the teacher moved out. Mr. Butler promised before he left that he would be back again in the fall, a relief to all of us. We had learned to rely on that little bit of income.

William missed him. He kept asking for "Mr. Buttle and 'is books." Mary tried to explain, but of course the time frame of "months" is difficult for a child to understand.

One midsummer afternoon I went for a long walk across my dreary-looking fields. The stalks were stunted and scarce. I plucked a head of grain here and there, chaffing it between my hands. There was nothing much there. I could feel the burden on my shoulders heavier with each step. There was nothing to harvest—again.

I crouched down in the field and dug at the ground with a stick, flipping back dry, dusty soil. Down, down I dug looking for moisture that was not there. Nothing. Why hadn't the rains come? What had happened to our world? *Seed time and harvest. Seed time and harvest* kept running through my head. God had promised it. Had He failed to deliver on His promise?

For a moment I was swept with anger. I was tempted to shake my fist at the heavens. What had I done to deserve this? What had Mary done? We had tried to be faithful. We—But I stopped myself. I knew it had nothing to do with that. Then the many years of trusting, of leaning on my Lord drained the anger from me.

"I need you, God," I whispered. "More than ever, I need you."

It was with heavy steps that I returned to the farmyard. I couldn't shake from me the feeling of impending doom. I had fought for about as long as I could fight. I didn't have much strength left.

After supper was over and the dishes returned to the cupboard, everyone settled in around the kitchen as usual. I tried to busy myself with figures and plans, but my mind wouldn't concentrate. I finally laid it all aside and climbed the stairs to the room where my two sons slept.

What a picture they made. William clutched the teddy bear that Sarah had made for his Christmas gift the year before. His dark lashes fell across unblemished cheeks and the thick brown hair lay damp across his forehead.

Baby Daniel slept in almost the same pose as his older brother—arms atop his blankets, his head held slightly to the side. But there was no teddy bear. Danny clutched only the hem of the blanket Mary had made. Now and then he pursed his little lips and took a few sucks as though he was dreaming of nursing.

I stood there looking at them both and the insides of me went cold and empty. *They're countin' on me. They're countin' on their pa, and I'm goin' to let them down. Both of them. Both of them—and Mary. And Grandpa and Uncle Charlie . . .*

I'd never experienced such pain. Deep, dark, knifing pain that brought no tears of relief.

I turned from my two sons and pulled the curtain back from the window so I could look out over the land I had loved and worked for so many years. There was no escaping it. We were facing the end.

I didn't even know Mary was there until she slipped her arms about my waist and laid her head against my upper back. A shudder went all through me.

She stood there for several minutes, just holding me, and then she spoke. Her voice was strong and even, though her words came to me in a soft whisper. "What is it, Josh? What's the matter?"

I had to get it out. Had to put it into words.

"We're gonna lose the farm," I said frankly, a cold harshness to my words.

Mary said nothing, but I felt her arms tighten around me.

William stirred in his sleep and his hand pulled the teddy more closely against him.

"It's the payments, isn't it? If you hadn't bought Pa's farm—"

Of course it was the payments. I stirred from one foot to the other in my impatience.

"I just made the wrong move—the wrong decision. I thought it was right—at the time—"

"No, Josh," Mary hastened to interrupt, "it wasn't wrong. Not the decision to buy. It was a wise thing to do. The *timin'* was just wrong, that's all. And no one—no one could have foreseen the future. Could have known how things would go. No rain—"

Grandpa had said the same thing, and in my head I knew they were right. But my heart? I had prayed. Had asked God about the purchase.

"Sell it, Josh," continued Mary. "Sell it."

"Can't sell it," I said, my voice now baring the impatience that my shifting feet had shown. "There's no one to buy."

"Then let it go. Just let it go. I know you sorta bought it for me—and our sons. But we'd be better—There will be other farms over the years. Maybe even Pa's again. We can buy later for the boys."

"I—I can't let it go," I protested hoarsely.

"Did you promise Pa? He'd understand, Josh. He'd not hold you to it."

"No, I didn't promise your pa. He didn't ask for a promise."

"Then let it go. Let the bank have it."

I turned then and took Mary by the shoulders, looking deeply into her eyes. There was no light on in the room, but the moon spilled through the window making her face light with a silvery glow. I could even see the faint scar across her forehead.

"You don't understand," I stated, with a great effort to keep my voice even. "If they take your pa's farm, they take this one too."

I felt Mary's body tremble.

"I signed them this, Mary. I signed it over to the bank when I took the loan. If I don't pay—"

But I'd said enough. Mary understood. She pressed herself into my arms and began to weep softly.

Maybe her crying helped us both. At least it brought some tenderness, some compassion back into the coldness of my heart. I stood holding her, caressing her, letting her cry.

It didn't last long and then Mary straightened her shoulders and lifted her chin.

"We've come too far to give up now," she said. "There *has* to be a way." I shrugged helplessly. Mary wiped her nose and went right on. "We still have stock to sell. The teacher will be back. I don't need all of his money for groceries. You can take out more cord wood, we'll—"

"Mary, we—"

"We'll make it," she repeated. "God has seen us through this far—He won't let us down now."

For a moment I found myself wondering just what God had done on our behalf. The rains still had not come. We hadn't had a crop in three years. But Mary soon reminded me.

"Folks all about have been losing their farms, but we still have ours. We been meetin' those payments year by year—somehow. We are all still here, all healthy. We've always had food on the table an' shoes on our feet. He's seen us through all of this, an' He'll keep right on providin'."

I felt a wave of shame rush through me. God had been doing far more for my family than I'd been thanking Him for.

"We'll make that next payment," said Mary again, her chin set firmly. She looked around the room. At me. At our two sons as they slept. "There's too much ridin' on it not to make it," she murmured in a half whisper; then I heard her simple, fervent prayer, "Help us, Lord, please help us."

We did make the payment. It was always a miracle to me. But we had to drain ourselves down to practically nothing to do it. We sold off almost all my good stock. I would have gladly sold the tractor and the Ford, but there were no buyers. What hurt the deepest was watching Chester go. We kept only the work horses because we simply could not get along without them. Chester brought a good price, even with the economy like it was. I could do nothing else but sell him. Mary cried, and I think I died a bit when the man came and led him away.

With all of that, I was still short for the bank payment. And then a letter came in the mail from Pa Turley. When Mary opened it, money fell to the kitchen table.

"This ain't much," he wrote, "but I hope that it helps in some way."

"Did you—?"

"No," Mary shook her head. "Really. I didn't say—"

The letter went on.

"Hear what a tough time everyone is having so I thought I'd send each of my girls a bit."

Mary laughed and cried at the same time. We added the bills to our little pile. It just met the bank payment.

Chapter 24

Striving to Make It

THERE WAS NOTHING MORE we owned that we could sell as far as I could see. We'd already spent all of Grandpa and Uncle Charlie's meager savings. The woodlot on the Turleys' farm was quickly being depleted. With so few vegetables and fruits canned or stored in the cellar, Mary's task of putting food before her family was very difficult and certainly would take a much larger portion of the teacher's board money. In fact, I didn't think she'd be able to make it stretch to do even that.

We had our backs against the wall, that was for sure. I began to make some inquiries in town about some kind of employment. As I feared, I could find nothing.

Then our whole community was shaken with a tragedy. We nearly lost Doc. Guess there wouldn't have been anyone in the whole neighborhood whose loss would have affected us more—unless it would have been my uncle Nat. Both men had been leaned on a lot during our hard times and looked up to a good deal during the better times we had experienced.

It was a heart attack. Doc was rushed off by motor car to the small hospital in Riverside. Mrs. Doc went right along with him and stayed by his bed to wait out the illness.

Doc had likely delivered everybody in the area, thirty-five and under. He'd sewed up cuts, taken out appendixes, nursed us through mumps and all sort of things. We'd miss him being there for us. Fact was, we didn't know how we'd ever get along without him. We all prayed daily that his life would be spared, even if his full health was not restored.

In the days following the heart attack, I kept thinking on the account I had with him. I owed Doc a considerable amount of money, and I had no way in the world to pay it. I was fearful that Mrs. Doc—we always called her that for some reason—I was afraid that she might be needing the money with the hospital bills and all, and I knew that the right thing to do was go and see her about it as soon as I had the chance, even if I didn't have the money. I could at least promise small payments just as soon as I could scrape something together.

In a few weeks' time news came that Mrs. Doc was back at the house in town, Doc having improved a good deal. I decided I'd best get on in and see her.

It was tough—but I made the call. Mrs. Doc looked a bit surprised to see me; then she welcomed me in like a long-lost son. I guess she felt that way about all the "babies" Doc had brought into the world.

After a bit of chitchat about Doc and how he was doing, I got right to the point.

"I came about my account," I said.

She seemed a bit bewildered.

"I was afraid that you might be needin' payment with Doc in the hospital an' all," I explained further.

She shook her head emphatically. "Oh, Doc would never leave me in need," she stated. "He made sure that he had everything cared for in case anything should happen. He's a good man, Doc is," and the tears started to form in her eyes.

Relieved to hear that they were not in dire straits, I told her, "I'll look after the account as soon as I'm able. Things are a bit tight right now, but I hope to get a job and then I can send some money month by month."

"There's nothing to pay, Josh," she told me softly.

"But there must be. I owe him a fair bit of money—Uncle Charlie, our baby. Just haven't been able to look after it yet."

Mrs. Doc went to a corner desk and withdrew a rather large ledger. "Come here," she said, and I went as bidden.

She leafed through the account book and I saw the names of our neighbors and friends listed there. They seemed to have fared better financially than the Joneses—I didn't spot a one of them who was owing Doc money. And then Mrs. Doc flipped another page and there was my name—Joshua Jones. Each entry was carefully made. Each sick call to our house and each of the deliveries, and the cost was clearly and carefully recorded in the column to the right. But it was the bottom of the page that made me gasp. There written beside the total was the distinct notation: "Paid in full."

"I—I don't understand," I stammered. "I didn't have money. Who—who—"

"Doc did," she said simply, the tears filling her eyes again. "The night of his attack. He must have known that something was wrong. He got up in the night. I found him here at his desk.

Cancelled out every account in the ledger—every debt—Doc did."

"But—but—"

She closed the book softly and slipped it back into the desk drawer.

"He loves his people, Josh. His community. He never wanted to take—just to give. He likely would never have taken payment if he hadn't been looking out for me. I'm cared for now, and he doesn't need any more."

I couldn't speak. All I could do was embrace the elderly woman. Then I returned to the brisk, cool air of the autumn day. I had much to think about as I trudged the street, still inquiring about work.

I heard about a government work project that was hiring. Mary hated the thought of it, for it would take me miles away from home and the family. We talked about it until way into the night and finally decided that it was the only thing we could do. With most of the stock gone, there wasn't much choring; and with no feed to speak of, the few remaining farm animals mostly had to forage for themselves anyway. Even Mary's chickens had been turned loose to fend for themselves. There still was a cow to milk, but Grandpa insisted that he could manage that.

With great reluctance I packed a few things in a carpet bag and prepared to take my leave. I wouldn't be needed at home for the next spring's planting. There was no seed grain in the bins—nor any hope of getting the money to buy any. I would just simply work out until our world had returned to normal again. And who knew just when that might be?

It was heart-wrenching to have me leave. Mary wept as she stuffed worn and oft-mended socks into a corner of the bag.

"They'll never get you through another winter," she sniffed. "They're nothin' but patches now."

"Where ya goin', Papa?" William asked, but the lump in my throat was too big for me to be able to answer him. I pulled the young boy into my arms and buried my face against his hair. He thought it was some kind of a game and started messing up my hair and tugging on my ears, squealing with glee. I wondered just how long it would be before I heard the boyish voice again. The thought made my chest constrict and brought tears to my eyes.

I continued to wrestle with William until I had myself under control. It was hard enough for Mary. I was supposed to be her strength.

We did the rounds with hugs. I guess it was the hardest moment of my life. William cried when he couldn't go with me. As I looked at little Daniel sleeping peacefully in his cradle, I tried to picture how big he'd be by the time I returned. I would miss so much of his growing up.

"Don't forget to write," reminded Mary for the third or fourth time. "I've packed the paper and envelopes in the side pocket there."

I nodded. I'd write. That would be all I'd have of home.

"Don't worry about things here," repeated Grandpa. "We'll manage just fine."

Oh, God, I groaned inwardly, *why does it have to be this way?*

Mary stepped out onto the cold back veranda for one final goodbye. She clutched her sweater tightly around her and turned to me with tears streaming down her cheeks.

"Don't worry, Josh," she whispered encouragingly in spite of the tears. "We'll manage—somehow."

I held her for a long time, trying to shield her from the cold, from the pain of parting and the heavy task of assuming all the responsibilities that I should be there to shoulder. *Why? Why?* I kept wondering, but the wind that whipped across the yard and tore at the weather-worn shutters had no answer.

"You'd best get in. You're freezing," I said to Mary, and I kissed her one last time and stumbled my way down the steps to the wagon. Grandpa was waiting to drive me to town to catch the local train.

I'd never realized how far it was to town before—nor how quickly our farm faded from view as we topped hill after hill.

The work camp was filled with men like myself. Desperate men—trying hard to make it through another winter in the only way that seemed open to them. Decent men—forwarding every penny they could spare back home to wives and family.

We talked about home in the evenings, after the work of another chilling, grueling day that numbed our bodies and tortured our muscles. We lay on our hard bunks and told one another stories about our wives, our children. It was the only pleasure we had. Except for the times when we allowed ourselves to use one more of our carefully rationed pages—one more envelope—one more stamp—so we could write a letter home. We lingered over those letters, savoring every word, pouring our love and longing into each sentence.

No one ever bothered a man who was writing. A hush fell over the bunkhouse and each man took to his bunk in respect for the one who held the hallowed position at the single, crude desk. Writing home was a sacred rite. It was as close to the family as we could get.

Mail day was even more special. We each hoarded every

speck of privacy as we pored over our letter. And then we did a strange thing—we went over and over every tiny item of news it held with everyone in the bunkhouse.

The work was difficult. I'd considered myself used to hard work, but this new thing—this swinging of a pick into hard-as-granite soil as we chopped to make way for a new canal across the arid, frozen prairie—was something quite new for me.

Many gave up and went home. Their backs simply could not endure the strain. It was never a problem for the job foreman when men quit. He had a long waiting list of men who yearned for a chance to put their bodies to the test and earn precious money for their families.

We had four days off for Christmas. Most of us walked the fifteen miles to town that night after putting in a full day's shift. We wanted to catch the train in the morning.

When the train pulled in to my familiar station, I stopped in town just long enough to buy a small trinket for each family member before I hoisted my bag and hurried home.

You should have heard the commotion. They hadn't known I was coming. We hugged and cried and hugged some more and everyone tried to talk at once, knowing full well that the time would pass too quickly for us to get everything said.

I couldn't believe how the boys had grown. I kept saying it to Mary over and over and she'd just smile.

We had a simple Christmas together with Lou's family. In spite of bare cupboard shelves, Lou and Mary managed to put together a tasty meal. The children didn't seem to miss the turkey and trimmings. They had fun just being together. That night Mary stayed up into the wee hours of the morning trying to darn my socks again. She patched my overalls and sewed buttons back on my coat, but there didn't seem to be much she could do about my worn-out mittens. The pick had been awfully hard on them.

"Josh," she said, "there's just no way to fix them."

I nodded. "They're fine," I assured her.

But the following morning when I joined the family at the breakfast table there was a new pair of mittens. She must have stayed up again most of the night in order to knit them. They were the same color as her chore sweater, which I noticed was no longer hanging on the peg by the door where she always kept it. I tried to swallow away the lump that grew large in my throat.

I left again right after breakfast. It was no easier than the first time. I had no idea when I'd be home again.

I guess it was my Bible and the time I was able to spend reading it and praying that got me through that long winter. Several other men in the bunkhouse turned to worn Bibles too. We talked about the things we were learning. It helped us to sorta put other things into proper perspective.

I told them about Willie one night. About how much he had loved God and how much I had loved him and how we had named our first son after him and all. They listened quietly.

"It's funny," I admitted. "He always went by 'Willie' even though his name was William. We named our boy in honor of him, and I think of Willie most every time I look at my son—and yet—yet—I've never been able to call him Willie. Never. Don't know why. Guess it still just hurts too much."

Heads nodded. I'd never been able to share that with anyone before. I guess I figured they wouldn't understand. But these men—there was a strange friendship between those of us who shared the simple, crude bunkhouse. Maybe because we were all so vulnerable. Maybe we had nothing to hide. We all knew just where the other one was coming from. None of us had reason or cause to boast. We were sorta laid bare, so to speak, before one another. And we needed one another.

I told them about Camellia too. Though I didn't bother to try to explain what Camellia had meant to me at one time. I just told them about Camellia and Willie and how she had gone out to Africa even after Willie had died there.

They were rightly impressed with Camellia.

And then I told them about the letter I'd had to write to the Mission Society, how it had been one of the hardest things I'd ever done in my life. How I'd told the Mission Society I just didn't have the money to support Camellia for the present and that just as soon as the rains came and I had another crop, I'd take up the support again.

A nice letter came back from them saying they understood and had managed to piece together Camellia's support from some other sources; but that hadn't taken the sting out of it for me.

"It's sure tough right now," mused a fella, Eb Penner. "Not just fer us, but fer the churches. I hear as how some missionaries have even been brought home. Jest no money."

"Hard fer the preachers, too," continued Paul Will. "Our parson hardly gits enough to git 'em by—an' he has 'im a family of seven. Grabs any job he can to make a dollar or two, an' so do his younguns—but ain't no work fer anybody."

"I stopped goin' to church," came from the corner bunk where Tom reclined, rubbing his hands as though he could work off some callouses. " 'Tweren't no comfort there, far as I could tell. Ever' Sunday, there was just more bad news of someone losin' their place or bein' outta food or some such. We was all asked to pray. I got tired of prayin'. Nothin' ever come of it anyway. Seemed I should be doin' more fer those in need than jest sayin' a prayer or two—an' I had nothin'—nothin' left to give."

No one in the room expressed shock. We'd all fought the same thoughts, the same feelings at one time or another.

"I kept on goin' anyway," admitted Eb. "I mighta felt a little helpless in the midst of my sufferin' brethren—but I'd a been downright lost without 'em."

"You see the collection plate?" Paul said. "Pittance. I don't know how any preacher's family can git by. Sure, a chicken here, a jug a milk there, but still I can't figure it. Tithe of nothin' is still nothin'."

The man was right of course. We'd always given our tithe. Even Mary's egg money was carefully counted and a tenth laid aside. But even at that we only dropped a few cents in on Sunday, and ofttimes there was nothing at all. We wondered, too, how Nat and Lou ever managed, but they made no complaints. God provided, Lou always said with a smile, but their clothes were threadbare and their table scantily served. It had been hard, all right, on those serving the churches.

"Well, one of these days it'll all get turned around again," said someone on a brighter note, and the conversation went in another direction. We all had great plans about what we'd do just as soon as the dry spell was over. For many it meant starting from the bottom again. They had already lost all they had. Businesses, farms, belongings. But still, to a man, we clung to that seemingly illusionary promise of the future.

I wrapped old rags around my hands to try to keep Mary's new mittens from developing holes. I wasn't worried about my bare hands on the cold pick handle. It was just that I couldn't stand the thought of ruining her gift to me—the mittens her love had kept her up all night to provide for me. The rags worked after a fashion, and then the weather finally began to warm up, and I tucked the mittens away and went barehanded. The frost left the ground, making the pick work a bit easier.

Being a farmer at heart, the melting of the ice and the warmth coming up from the soil sent my blood to racing. It was hard for me to keep my eyes off the skies. If only—if only the rains would come.

But even if they do, I reminded myself, *I'll still need to stay with my pick and shovel.* I had not been able to save even a few pennies. I sent all that I made back to Mary and the family so they could get by.

Chapter 25

Another Spring, Another Promise

THAT NIGHT I WROTE another letter to Mary. I seemed to get more and more lonesome with each passing day. Would the ache in my heart never ease? I had thought that it would get easier with time. It hadn't. Not at all.

After I'd written my letter, I lay on my bunk for a long time just thinking. Then I took my Bible and began to leaf through it, looking for some kind of comfort in its pages. I read a number of Mary's Psalms and they helped, but I was still aching with the intensity of my loneliness.

I need my family, I kept saying over and over to myself. *I need Mary.*

But I was caught in a box. If I went home to Mary I would surely lose the farm. Even if I wasn't able to save anything for the bank loan, my being here away from my family would sow "good faith," I reasoned. Yet I wondered how much longer I could hold on here. If only—if only God would provide some way for me to make those payments—to hold the land. If only—if only the rains would come so the land could produce again.

I started praying. "God," I admitted, "I'm at the end of myself. There's nothin' that Josh Jones can do to provide for a future—any future for Mary, for my sons. I can hardly provide for the present. I don't know which way to turn, Lord. I just don't know how we can go on like this. I need them. They need me. But to lose the farm. What would we do then? Where would we go? We have nothin', Lord. Nothin'."

The Bible slipped from my fingers and rested on the bunk beside me. I picked it up and held it to my chest for a moment, thinking and praying silently, then I shifted it back to read again. My eyes fell to the page that had opened before me. At some time in my growing years I must have read the passage, for it was underlined as though it had impressed me. I read it again now.

> Although the fig tree shall not blossom,
> neither shall fruit be in the vine;
> the labour of the olive shall fail,
> and the fields shall yield no meat;
> the flock shall be cut off from the fold,
> and there shall be no herd in the stalls.
> Yet I will rejoice in the Lord,
> I will joy in the God of my salvation.
> The Lord God is my strength.

I reread the passage again and again until the tears that filled my eyes prevented me from reading it further.

It was all coming clear to me. The welfare of my family didn't depend on my strength. If so, they would be utterly destitute.

I had been totally inadequate. But even more astounding, it didn't depend upon my fields either, or the herds that I had so carefully built. It was God all the time—just like Mary had tried to tell me. It was God who had cared for my family—had met their needs. We didn't need anyone or anything else.

" 'I will rejoice in the Lord—the Lord God is my strength,' " I kept repeating over and over. Oh, what a freedom! I could finally let go. I could shift my heavy load onto another's shoulders. Somehow—somehow God would work it out. Somehow He would see us through. Maybe we *wouldn't* keep the farm—but if not—well, He'd help us to manage without it. Somehow!

By now soft snoring reached to me from the other bunks and I knew the men around me were getting much-needed rest. Yet I continued to inwardly pray and praise until late into the night. When I rose the next morning, it was with new strength.

When I picked up my pick and shovel and fell into line, the task had not changed—but my attitude had. God was in charge now—I would simply wait for Him. But for now—for now I was on the payroll of the government. They expected a full day's work. All through the morning the sound of rhythmic blows sounded on the gravelly banks around me. The work continued on the irrigation canal gradually worming its way across the barren and desolate prairie land. By this time in the season, the sun had climbed higher in the sky and beat on our backs with intensity, making us sweat heavily with each swing of the pick or scoop of the shovel. Men complained of the heat as ferociously as they had complained about the cold.

"Wish it would rain," grumbled a voice to my right. "Sure would be a relief from this dust." I wasn't the only one who often lifted his eyes to the sky, but still no clouds formed.

I lifted my pick again to let it strike the ground with a dull thud. My back ached, my shoulders ached, my arms ached. I was about to swing again when a voice stopped me. Someone was calling my name.

"Jones," I heard again. "You're wanted."

I hoisted my pick and shovel and followed the beckoning hand. One never dared leave tools behind. You were useless on the job without them, and there simply was no money to replace them should they disappear.

"The phone!" shouted the messenger. "Over in the foreman's shack."

I flipped my pick and shovel over my shoulder and started at a jog for the building, my insides churning. Who would be phoning me and what possible message could they have?

With a trembling hand I picked up the receiver. There was a crackling in my ear.

"Hello!" I hollered into the mouthpiece.

"He—lo," came back a broken response. It was Grandpa. My whole body froze. Something must be terribly wrong. He wouldn't squander money on a telephone call unless it was extremely important.

"That you, Boy?"

"It's—it's me. Josh," I managed.

"Hang on!" yelled Grandpa.

I was about mad with anxiety. Why would he call me and then say "hang on"? Then another voice came on the line.

"Josh?" It was Mary. I felt great relief. At least Mary was all right.

"Josh?" she said again.

"Mary! Mary, what's—"

"It's raining, Josh." Silence. "It's raining."

I looked out at the clear, hot afternoon sky. There wasn't a cloud in sight. No—wait! Way to the northwest I could see clouds against the distant horizon.

"It settled in right over us. It's been raining for three days now. I waited to call until I was sure it wasn't just a shower. I—" But then Mary began to weep.

There was a bit of a pause and next thing Grandpa was on the line again. "Rainin', Boy," he informed me. "Third day. Just comin' down like ya haven't seen in years." He chuckled. "Clouds still hangin' over us. We near got drowned comin' into town."

"Sun's still shining here," I managed to reply. I was trembling now, still hardly able to believe the report.

"Maybe it'll move yer way after it's finished with us," Grandpa chortled.

Then he spoke words that I will never forget. "Come home, Boy," he said.

"Come home?"

I heard him swallow. "We already got some crop in."

"Crop?"

"Yep."

"Who?"

"Mary an' me. Some of it's showin' already. This rain will really bring it."

"How'd you—? Where'd you get the seed?" I floundered.

"Bought it."

"Bought it *how*? Where'd you get the money?" I asked, unable to grasp what Grandpa was saying.

"Mary gathered it—somehow—she's been savin' pennies. Little bit each month from what you've sent. I don't know how she did it, but she managed to git herself quite a little pile."

"But surely that wasn't enough to—" I could imagine the small bit of seed those few dollars would buy.

"Well," confessed Grandpa, "she—she also sold the silver tea service."

"What? Where?"

"Some lady—out-of-towner. Seemed to want it real bad. Took a mighty fancy to it. Paid a good price, Mary said."

I was too stunned to speak. I knew how much that tea set had meant to Mary. For a moment I just stood there, thoughts whirling round and round as I tried to take in everything Grandpa was telling me. The silver tea set—gone. Mary saving, planting. A crop already in the ground and growing. It was all too much—too much for me.

The realization of the cost of the call finally got me talking again. "Is she still there? Mary?" I asked.

"Yep," and I heard Grandpa hand her the phone.

"Mary?"

"Yes." Her voice was no more than a whisper.

"Mary, I'm coming home."

There was only a little sob, caught somewhere in Mary's throat.

"I'm leavin'—I'm leavin' right now."

"Oh, Josh," sobbed Mary.

"Mary—I love you."

I hung up the receiver then and turned to the foreman at the desk. "I'm leavin'," I informed him. "I'm going to pack up my gear and will be right back to pick up my pay. Someone else can have my spot on the crew."

He nodded. It was done 'most every week. An exchange made.

I ran all the way to the bunkhouse. I was going home!

I'm goin' home! I exulted. *Back to my wife—my Mary. Back to my family. Back to my farm.* We hadn't lost it. The rains had come. Sure, things were tough. Sure, we had a ways to go in order to rebuild, but we still had our home—our land. We were going to have another chance. God was giving us another chance for seedtime—and harvest!

Epilogue

THOUGH THE STORY OF Josh and his family has been totally fictional, readers like to feel that they know a little about what happens to the characters in the future. So let's travel on and add a bit to the family story.

Though the years following the drought were difficult for the Jones family, Josh eventually became known as the best and most prosperous farmer in the area. But with the increase in crop production and the rebuilding of his herds, Josh never did flaunt or waste his wealth. Besides Camellia in Africa, he eventually shared in the support of nine other missionaries.

To the family were born six children. William and Daniel were joined by Andrew, Violet, Irene, and Walter. Andrew was the one to farm the Turley home place. And like his father and mother before him, he too became actively supportive of missionaries, among whom were three members of his own family. William went to Sierra Leone, Violet to Japan, while Daniel pastored a small mission church among the Canadian Indians. Irene married Phillip Moresby, the son of the doctor who came to take Doc's place. Phillip trained as a physician and joined his father in the family practice. Walter, Josh and Mary's youngest, eventually was lost in the Korean war.

All five of the remaining Jones children married. To Josh and Mary were born twenty-three grandchildren, and they saw the arrival of seventeen great-grandchildren to bless their old age.

Grandpa lived to be ninety-six, but Uncle Charlie left behind his arthritis-ridden body at the age of seventy-four.

The family has scattered now. With the passing of time and the mobility of our age, they no longer cluster about the home farm. Where do they live? Well—here and there. Perhaps—just perhaps—you share your neighborhood with some of them.

Books by Janette Oke

Acts of Faith*

The Centurion's Wife • The Hidden Flame

Canadian West

When Calls the Heart • When Comes the Spring
When Breaks the Dawn • When Hope Springs New
Beyond the Gathering Storm
When Tomorrow Comes

Love Comes Softly

Love Comes Softly • Love's Enduring Promise
Love's Long Journey • Love's Abiding Joy
Love's Unending Legacy • Love's Unfolding Dream
Love Takes Wing • Love Finds a Home

A Prairie Legacy

The Tender Years • A Searching Heart
A Quiet Strength • Like Gold Refined

Seasons of the Heart

Once Upon a Summer • The Winds of Autumn
Winter Is Not Forever • Spring's Gentle Promise
Seasons of the Heart (4 in 1)

Song of Acadia*

The Meeting Place • The Sacred Shore • The Birthright
The Distant Beacon • The Beloved Land

Women of the West

The Calling of Emily Evans • Julia's Last Hope
Roses for Mama • A Woman Named Damaris
They Called Her Mrs. Doc • The Measure of a Heart
A Bride for Donnigan • Heart of the Wilderness
Too Long a Stranger • The Bluebird and the Sparrow
A Gown of Spanish Lace • Drums of Change

www.janetteoke.com

*with Davis Bunn